THE JACKSON RAID

The bank in the town of Jackson was claimed to be beyond the wit and guile of any man to rob. However, no one had reckoned on the audacious planning of Miras Carter, whose bid to disprove the claim knew no limits. Meanwhile, Duke Mason and his gang's quest for bank riches stood or fell in the blaze of fast guns. There was destined to be a violent and deadly climax when the two gangs clashed. For Sheriff Frank Malley, though, the problem was: could he stay alive?

LUTHER CHANCE

THE JACKSON RAID

Complete and Unabridged

LINFORD
Leicester

First published in Great Britain in 2001 by
Robert Hale Limited
London

First Linford Edition
published 2003
by arrangement with
Robert Hale Limited
London

British Library CIP Data

Chance, Luther
    The Jackson raid.—Large print ed.—
Linford western library
    1. Western stories
    2. Large type books
    I. Title
    823.9′14 [F]

ISBN 0–7089–4917–7

Published by
F. A. Thorpe (Publishing)
Anstey, Leicestershire

Set by Words & Graphics Ltd.
Anstey, Leicestershire
Printed and bound in Great Britain by
T. J. International Ltd., Padstow, Cornwall

This book is printed on acid-free paper

This one for B and P

1

They said of the town that if you wanted to die young, Jackson was the place to be. They also said of the settlement that it was the fastest growing, wealthiest, sassiest town south of Laramie Peaks. There were those, of course, who reckoned Jackson for the meanest town they had ever crossed, but they had no stomach for pressing the opinion.

Jackson had prospered on the thriving stage route skirting the salt lakes to the sweeping plains out Campsville way. Later, as the railroad had driven relentlessly West, it had boomed to a thriving cattle head.

The town had hotels, bars, gambling saloons, mercantiles, a saddlery, gunsmith, livery, butchers, tailors, barbers, classy girl houses, a healthy string of busy whores, law and order in the shape of Sheriff Frank Malley, and was home to Circuit Judge Maitland McArthur.

It was also the headquarters of the Western Central and South Peaks Bank, a fact that any new arrival in town could not fail to overlook as he made his way along the bustling main street.

Dominating the variety of stylish buildings was the imposing façade and decorated bulk housing the bank's business counters, offices and vaults where more than twenty over-managers, under-managers, clerks, tellers, trainees, odd job lackeys and scrubbed flunkies greased the wheels of the money market of those for whom, as the Western Central and South Peaks proudly proclaimed, 'We are destined only to serve with honour, integrity and selfless devotion'.

To which founder, life president and undisputed factotum of the bank, Louis Thorneybank Reuben Quainsley, would have added, 'and earn as much goddamn profit as we can make look half decent!'

Pausing for a moment at the bank's double doors, the new arrival would similarly not fail to notice the strength and depth of the security displayed.

Never less than four frock-coated, armed men were positioned to pace and stay alert along the boardwalk out front; there to watch, observe and protect, and, when deemed necessary, 'detain anyone acting in a manner likely to impede or prejudice the operations of the bank'.

This dictum also applied to the guards positioned on the business floor and within the vicinity of the vaults and strongrooms; a total in all of some ten hard-bitten, mean-eyed gunslingers on the personal payroll of the president.

These men, under the captaincy of Hank Scots, were never to have their orders or actions questioned by anyone. It was just one of the many unwritten 'laws' of Jackson declared by Louis Quainsley. And nobody questioned him either.

And so the new arrival would pass

on, resolved that should the time ever come when he attained the status of a man of means and property he would not hesitate to invest his wealth with the Western Central and South Peaks Bank.

'Nobody in his right mind would ever figure — or so much as get to thinkin' to figure — robbin' such a bank,' the new arrival would claim with pride and conviction. 'Could never be done.'

Could it?

2

Of Jackson's two hotels — the Silver Palace and the Plainsman — the Palace was by far the larger, more luxurious and certainly more expensive. Here, as distinct from the Plainsman with its earthy approach to pretty well everything, the Palace boasted silks, brocades, the finest porcelain, *objets-d'art*, furniture from back East (some of it 'a real genuine antique') fashionable taste and the raw evidence of money. Leastways, this had always been proprietor Bertram Carbonne's policy and intent.

'Folks resident at the Palace are here on business — coming from it, going to it — and the cost of their accommodation ain't of the slightest concern. Palace clients don't give money a second thought . . . '

Just so, just so, Jake Haston, Palace

reception desk clerk, reckoned on that warm, cloudless, sunlit afternoon in July, as he booked Miss Geraldine Dreyfus into a front-facing luxury suite for an 'indeterminate period pending the arrival by rail of my fiancé from Montana.'

Jake figured that if the lady's fiancé had anything about him he would make that journey south at one hell of a lick. Who would want to leave a woman of her class and beauty alone in an hotel room for longer than a day? And not that if he had any sense.

By contrast on that same afternoon, but on the other side of the street — the two-bit side where the drunks cluttered the shade and the off-duty whores took a breather — Gus Chappell swept a lazy besom through the deserted lounge of the Plainsman and wondered how it was that the fellow who had just booked in had insisted on a street-facing room with a big window.

Takes all sorts, he had mused, blinking into the slow cloud of dust that drifted to the open door, and he figured for having seen most of them pass through the Plainsman, but this fellow, who had arrived on the noon stage and signed in as Oliver Adams, Wyoming, was something a mite unexpected.

Neat, dapper, well dressed in a smart tweed suit, polished shoes, button spats, quiet spoken, twitchy smile, with a tendency to heavy sweating at the brow and gills. One piece of luggage, an expensive leather case. The sort of fellow more at home in the glitter of the Palace than the gloom of the dusty Plainsman.

Still, he had paid up front for a week and nobody looked ready money in the face. He could have his room — *any* room, come to that — and spend the whole darned week at the window if it suited.

There was little enough of a view: the Palace, Benjamin Bright's sprawling emporium and mercantile, Miss Peabody's millinery, Joe Acorn's saddlery, the bank, Doc Baynam's surgery, the staging office and, if you stretched real hard to the left, Polly Sweet's gaming and girl house.

Mr Oliver Adams, of Wyoming, was welcome to as much of it as he could take in!

Gus grunted, settled his besom and leaned thoughtfully on the long handle. Even so, he reflected, he would report the arrival of the fellow to Sheriff Malley as was required and deemed the 'law' by Louis Quainsley.

'No strangers in town without I know to them,' had been the sheriff's edict on the instructions, naturally, of the bank's president.

Within an hour of you hitting town, Malley would know who you were, where you were staying and for how long, where you had come from and what your business in Jackson was about.

Your stay in town would be monitored by deputies; your movements, where you ate, drank and who you slept with duly noted. And when you finally left, the detail of that too would be recorded in Sheriff Malley's book of visitors. There were no exceptions, no mistakes made.

Not until that cloudless, sunlit day in July, anyhow.

★ ★ ★

Polly Sweet had an eye for trouble. It came of long experience and a few harsh lessons at the hands of the scum-bag drifters, no-hopers, chancers, layabouts, gamblers and misfits she generally had to deal with in her house of gaming, girls and cheap booze.

All in a day's work, a part of the scene. Some fellow strode in, weeks of trail dirt and stench in his wake, took a bath (that was a house rule) cleaned up best he could on what he had — usually little more than a moth-eaten bedroll — took his drink, chose his game and his girl and paid up before he got started on either of them. Another house rule.

But today, in the heat, with the sun high, the sky empty, the flies dozing and business on the ebb of siesta and the main street quiet for the hour, things were shaping up different.

Take that fellow there at the corner table, thought Polly, for the tenth time in as many minutes, now just what was with him? Hardly the type she normally had to handle: smart suit, quality boots, fine hat, carved buckle belt and a holstered Colt that looked classy enough, but you could bet the fellow knew only too well how to use it. And had. Many times.

And another thing, how come the fellow had been so keen to introduce himself? Most men crossing the threshold into Polly's parlour were only too anxious to keep their identity strictly under wraps. Not this one . . .

'Name's Chad Lawton,' he had said through an attractive smile, as he had doffed his hat and taken Polly's hand. 'Just stepped down from the stage, ma'am, and real pleased to meet yuh I am.'

Well, he might be, and she in truth was not averse to a shot of decent manners and sweet-smelling breath around the place for once. Made a real nice change. But Chad Lawton — what sort of a name was that, save one dreamed up?

'Welcome to Jackson, Mr Lawton,' Polly had responded, with an equally ready smile, her hand still in the man's grip. 'Business, or just passin' through?'

'Oh, I'd guess yuh'd say passin' through. Coupla days or so.' And still holding her hand in his, had added, 'I don't suppose you could accommodate me here for that short while, could you?'

'Two hotels in town, mister. Count your cash and pay your price.' Polly had finally removed her hand. 'We don't do beds here — leastways not on a permanent basis, if yuh follow me.'

Lawton's smile had broadened. 'Of course,' he said generously.

'Cut a deck and you can play most any game,' Polly had said. 'And my girls are the best. Don't come cheap, but they're the best. We stay open most nights 'til sun up. This time of day is slow, but yuh welcome to what yuh see.'

'All of what I see?' Lawton had chuckled with a wink.

'That sorta talk flatters, but it don't pay the bills. Help yourself to a drink from the bottle there. Cards are on the tables. Girls come on at six.'

And there he had sat ever since, a game of Patience drifting slowly through his fingers, only occasionally breaking his concentration to smile, wink provocatively and go back to the cards.

So what, wondered Polly again, was Mr Chad Lawton really doing in town? Who was he, where had he come from, and why had he avoided booking into an hotel in the first place? She was going to have few answers to report to Sheriff Malley when the time came.

Fellows like Lawton could spell trouble. She had heard the smooth-talking before, seen the smart suits, but it was the Colt that troubled her the most. Minute he got to drawing on a piece that classy —

And then the gunfire from somewhere in the street ripped apart the quiet of that afternoon.

★ ★ ★

Polly Sweet reached the boardwalk from her parlour four steps ahead of Chad Lawton and just in time to save the milliner, Miss Peabody, from a headlong sprawl in the dirt.

Joe Acorns tumbled from his saddlery to a mêlée of passers-by suddenly huddled in a tight, chattering group. Gus Chappell shouldered his besom and dashed into the shadowed side of the street only to be thrown back by the vicious blaze of more gunshots as a Winchester-toting drunk in a rag-bag assortment of clothes weaved and staggered his way towards the Palace hotel.

'Where the devil he come from?'

13

yelled a man from the shade.

'Somebody go get the sheriff.'

'Yeah, where the hell's the law round here?'

The drunk blazed another round of shots and swung the rifle through a threatening arc. 'First one to move gets holed,' he slurred. 'Yuh hear? Holed. And I ain't for foolin' one bit.'

Miss Peabody fainted in Polly Sweet's arms. The bank guards closed menacingly. Joe Acorns squinted behind his sweat. Gus Chappell swallowed and almost snapped his besom in his frozen grip. Hitched mounts began to buck and snort. A man shouted obscenities. A woman screamed and passed out.

But it was Chad Lawton, Colt drawn in a steady hand, who approached the drunk on his blind side and before the fellow could stagger another step, clubbed him to the ground, collected the Winchester and calmly scattered its remaining ammunition to the dirt.

Only then, with Sheriff Malley and two deputies arriving in a flurry of waving arms, did he turn to face the Plainsman and the largest window overlooking the street.

The man watching from it merely nodded.

3

'Nice goin', mister. Yuh did well there; saw the situation and reacted fast. I like that in a man. Grateful to yuh.' Sheriff Frank Malley blew a long, thin shaft of cigar smoke to the nicotine-stained ceiling of his office, leaned back in his chair and stared hard into the pale blue eyes watching him. 'Yuh know this fella we brought in by any chance, Mr Lawton?'

'Never clapped eyes on him before,' said Lawton, his gaze straying beyond the sheriff to the still unconscious body sprawled on the cell bunk. 'Can't say he's exactly the type I'd wanna get close to.' He sniffed and winced.

'Well, he won't be doin' a deal of talkin' for a while yet,' murmured Malley. 'Some clout you gave him.'

'I wasn't for debatin' the issue,' gestured Lawton. 'Another minute and the rat might've got to killin' some-body.'

Malley grunted and blew more smoke. 'Drunk as a coot. Cheap hooch and no stomach for it. We get 'em time to time. Drift in off the plains, outa the woods — but this one, hell, he stinks real bad. Must've been livin' rough for months.' He wafted a hand across the smoke cloud. 'Odd thing is, though, he stabled one helluva good-lookin' horse at the livery.' He paused a moment to glance at his deputies lounging either side of the door. 'And that Winchester, some piece, eh, boys?'

'Say that again, boss,' drawled one of the men, examining his fingernails. 'He for sure as hell didn't *buy* it, you can bet on that.'

Lawton slapped his knees, pushed back the chair and came to his feet. 'I guess that's goin' to be your problem, Sheriff,' he grinned lightly. 'Me, I'm only too glad to have been of service to your good town. And now, if yuh don't mind, I fancy gettin' back to the girls and a game of cards.'

'Where yuh stayin', Mr Lawton?' asked Malley.

'Well, now, I ain't rightly got to that little matter,' smiled Lawton. 'Fact is, Sheriff, I was sorta plannin' on roomin' with the lady back there at the gamin' house, but she didn't seem overly taken with the suggestion, gentle as it was, so mebbe I'll just — '

'There'll be a room for you at the Palace whenever you're ready. Compliments of the town. Least we can do. Ask for Carbonne.' The sheriff blew softly on the tip of his cigar. 'Will yuh be stayin' long, Mr Lawton?' he murmured, his gaze lifting slowly.

'Coupla days or so. Got some business at the bank, then I'll be gone.' Lawton's smile widened. 'Meantime, I'm mightily obliged to you for the town's generosity. I call that real friendly. Yessir, real friendly.' He adjusted his hat. 'Hope yuh find the fella talkative when he comes to. Thanks again. Meantime, I'll bid yuh good day.'

Sheriff Malley waited a full two minutes after Chad Lawton had stepped back to the street and closed the office door behind him before blowing another cloud of smoke and turning to his deputies.

'That fella ain't for real,' he said, leaning forward. 'One of yuh check him out. Follow him. I wanna know all there is to know. And if he gets to drawin' that fancy Colt again, take it from him.' He came to his feet. 'You want me, I'm at the Palace.'

The sleeping drunk in the cell stirred and moaned, but nobody noticed his eyes were open.

* * *

Geraldine Dreyfus lifted her long, silk-stockinged leg to place her foot on the stool, slid the pearl-handled derringer into her frilly garter, swept her skirt back into position and smiled softly to herself.

It was all going very well; neat, tidy, no snags and to time. Almost perfect, though best not to be too presumptuous, she thought, smoothing the folds of the skirt again as she crossed the elegantly furnished and ornately decorated room to the window overlooking the main street.

Yes, she mused, all going well: Oliver Adams in position at the Plainsman, Chad Lawton playing his part with his usual style in the carefully staged arrest of Red James, and soon, she surmised, to be safely installed here in the Palace, the sheriff convinced and suitably impressed with his single-handed, heroic performance. Highly satisfactory. Now, it needed only Carter to arrive and the brains of the team would be assembled.

She murmured on a deeper thought and glanced at the clock on the dressing-table. No consolation to be found there; it would be another whole day before the train carrying Carter from Montana reached Jackson. She sighed, turned from the window and crossed to the bed.

She would rest a while, she decided, get to mulling over the finer details of the plan, be sure they had not overlooked anything, rehearse it again and again in her mind. And think of Carter at her side.

Geraldine Dreyfus was still sound asleep when the late afternoon light finally faded.

* * *

'Can't tell yuh a thing yuh don't already know, Frank. Fella blew into town on the stage, stepped down along of the others, that good-looking woman I got in number seventeen included, and that was that.'

Bertram Carbonne shrugged, dusted a drift of cigar ash from his brocade waistcoat and strolled possessively round his lavishly furnished private office at the Silver Palace Hotel.

'Next thing I knew,' he went on, 'the fella was settlin' that two-bit drunk in no uncertain terms. Good thing he did, too. Could've gotten nasty.' He dusted at another drift of ash, halted at the full-length mirror on the wall facing the door, and preened himself fussily. 'Lucky for you I had a room for him. Not that I mind, yuh understand. Yuh did the right thing rewardin' him like that. Fella's one heap grateful. Out there now in the bar.'

'I know, I seen him,' murmured Sheriff Malley from his seat at the baize-topped table. 'He gettin' drinks on the house?'

'Hmmm, one or two,' shrugged Carbonne. 'Just to show a civic appreciation. Barman knows when to call a halt. Meantime, yuh help yourself, Frank. Bottle's there in front of yuh. Only the best.'

Malley grunted and poured himself a generous measure. 'Fella say much?' he asked, slapping his lips.

'Not a deal. Just went to his room — number four at the back — washed, changed, then headed for the bar. Said he was here on business at the bank. Be around a couple of days. Next stop somewhere south. Out San Ramon way, I think he said.'

Malley gulped on the drink. 'New arrival at the Plainsman, I hear.'

'Gus Chappell figures him for a salesman. Fussy type. Keepin' to his room.' Carbonne tweaked the curl of his sideburns and turned from the mirror. 'Lawton's the gamblin' type if yuh want my opinion. Sharp eye for the ladies, too, I shouldn't wonder. Might be well-lined financially; could just as easily be a con. Quainsley'll spot it either way, don't you fret.'

'Mebbe,' said Malley finishing the drink, then coming to his feet. 'Yuh keep your eyes peeled, yuh hear?'

'There won't be no trouble, Frank,' smiled Carbonne. 'I seen all types through here, and Lawton don't rate none. He'll drink his fill, have himself a woman and be sittin' in Quainsley's office come mornin' with one helluva head! You see if he ain't.' He adjusted his waist-coat expansively. 'Now, if it's interestin' folk yuh lookin' for, the lady in number seventeen, Miss Geraldine Dreyfus — '

There was a tap at the door.

'It's open,' called Carbonne, turning back to the mirror as Malley's deputy, hat in fidgeting hands, scraped his way into the room and looked anxiously at the sheriff. 'We got trouble, boss,' he croaked.

'What sorta trouble?' drawled Malley.

'That bank guard, Hank Scots . . . Somebody's gone and slit his throat back of Polly Sweet's place. Still bleedin' like a hog, but very dead.'

Bertram Carbonne winced as he pulled at a loose hair in a sideburn.

Sheriff Malley was tempted to pour himself another drink, but could only break into a cold, clinging sweat.

4

A stunned, murmuring crowd had gathered outside Polly Sweet's gaming house and was spreading in its curiosity into the alley that led to the rear by the time Sheriff Malley and his deputy arrived on the scene.

'That'll do, folks,' he called, bustling his way into the gathering with a firm but friendly hand on straining shoulders, a gentle smile to the women who huddled among themselves. 'I'm sure there ain't nothin' here as yuh really wanna see. Leave this to the law, eh? Me and my man here'll soon have the critter who did it brought to book, yuh can rest on that.'

'What the hell was the fella doin' back there, anyhow?' piped a voice from somewhere in the thick of the crowd.

'If yuh gotta ask a question like that, Charlie Timms, at a place like Polly

Sweet's, there ain't no hope for yuh!' came an answer to a burst of titters and jeers.

'Shouldn't be allowed,' shrilled a voice from the huddle of townswomen. 'Place should've been closed long back.'

'Then where's yuh husband goin' to spend his nights, lady?' cracked a lounging man.

'Well, really,' huffed another woman, pulling at her long gloves, 'such an attitude — '

'If yuh ain't comin' in, why don't yuh all go home?' snapped Polly Sweet, bustling across the boardwalk in a swirl of skirts and waving arms, two of her girls trailing in her wake. Her eyes gleamed in the lantern-smoothed shadows. 'Well, what yuh gawpin' at, f'Cris'sake? I ain't the one with the skeletons in the cupboard! Tell yuh somethin' else — '

'All right, Polly, all right,' soothed Malley, reasserting his authority, 'they got the message. No cause to spoil for a fight. We've got enough on our hands.'

He turned to the wide-eyed, sweat-faced crowd. 'Do like Polly says, eh, get yourselves home? There ain't nothin' yuh can do, and there ain't goin' to be nothin' to see.' He eased closer to his deputy. 'Take over. I'm goin' to the bank. Doc Baynam here yet?'

'With the body now,' grunted the man. 'Some of Hank's bank friends along of him.'

'Just keep this lot right here, yuh understand?' said Malley, then turning to Polly Sweet added, 'You'd best come with me, gal. Yuh'll be a sight safer with the dead than the livin' right now.'

* * *

'Took a blow from the butt of a gun — Colt very likely — before whoever it was killed him finished it with a knife.' Doc Baynam sniffed, blinked his tired eyes into focus beneath a forest of bushy brows, closed his medicine bag and stared intently into Sheriff Malley's face. 'Quick, clean, clinical. Fella who

27

did this had done it before.' He sniffed again and twitched his eyebrows. 'Yuh lookin' for a cold killer.'

Sheriff Malley grunted thoughtfully as his gaze probed the dark, shadowed clutter of the back alley and came to rest on the already stiffening body of Hank Scots sprawled in a pool of congealing blood.

'Any ideas?' he said to the two bank security guards at his side. 'He get to cultivatin' enemies all of a sudden?'

'Yuh make 'em fast in the bankin' job,' drawled one of the men, rolling a wad of tobacco round his mouth. 'Mebbe he had more than most, but he never said. Could've mentioned somethin' to Quainsley, o'course.' He sucked on the wad and spat. 'Yuh want my opinion, he was messin' with some other fella's woman.'

Malley's gaze moved to Polly Sweet. 'Yuh know anythin' of this, Poll?' he asked quietly.

'Nope,' said Polly Sweet flatly, folding her arms under the covers of the shawl at her shoulders. 'T'ain't no secret Hank was a reg'lar customer. So what? Don't go to say he was deep with one of the girls. We don't encourage it. Bad for business. No, the way I see it — '

'When you've all done opinionizin' and before yuh get to puttin' it to a town vote,' growled Doc with a flourish of his bag, 'I'll tell yuh somethin' about our killer — seein' as how yuh seem to have overlooked it.' He sniffed loudly. 'Yuh smell anythin'?' he asked.

'Usual town dirt,' mouthed one of the guards.

'Scented water,' said Doc with another flourish of his bag. 'Sort of thing some fancy dude fellas slap across their cheeks when they're all through shavin'. Ask Herbie at the barbers'. He'll tell yuh.'

'Doc's right, I can smell it,' said Polly.

'Well, now yuh come to mention it . . . ' began the second guard.

'It's for a fact that Hank ain't wearin' no such scent,' continued Doc, 'so I figure for it bein' whoever was here not a half-hour back.'

'And now I come to think on it,' added Polly, unfolding her arms to adjust the shawl, 'there was the same smell when I stepped out the back and found the body. Never rated it then.'

Malley cleared his throat and grunted, 'So I'm lookin' for a sweet-smellin' fella, who shaved around sundown. That it?'

'A *stranger* who shaved about sundown,' said Doc with a wink.

'Oh, and how'd yuh figure for him bein' a stranger?' asked Malley.

''Cus I happen to know that Herbie don't stock no such scented water, not of this smell, anyhow.' Doc Baynam tightened his grip on his bag. 'Fella wearin' the scent yuh can smell is carryin' his own supply, which, to my reckonin', kinda points to him bein' new in town. A stranger. A visitor. Narrows the field a deal, don't it? Tell yuh somethin' else — '

Doc fell silent at a sudden surge of

shouts and yelling in the main street.

'What the hell — ?' hissed Malley, spinning on his heel.

'Yuh there, Sheriff?' came the cry across the darkness. 'Yuh'd best get out here — that fella yuh jailed a while back has just sprung himself! Cell's empty and there ain't a hair nor hide of the scumbag nowheres. And yuh deputy's dead.'

The sweat in Malley's neck began to freeze.

★   ★   ★

The summons came one hour and twenty minutes before midnight.

Sheriff Frank Malley noted the time on the clock in his office with care; it was important to be precise and attend to the detail in any negotiation with Louis Quainsley, who had made a fortune, he claimed, by 'keeping his head and keeping to time'.

But on this night his head was sore and time was pressing.

'I ain't for beatin' about the back-woods over this, Malley,' he clipped, as if spitting the words through honed teeth, 'but this sorta trouble in our town — *my* town — is not what I treble your salary for every month. What's the latest?'

Quainsley lit a large cigar, blew an angry cloud of thick smoke and began a slow, measured pacing of his luxuriously furnished private quarters above the business area of the Western Central and South Peaks bank. His gaze, narrowed and seemingly unblinking, was annoyingly averted from the watchful faces of Sheriff Malley and Circuit Judge Maitland McArthur, seated at the heavy oval table where a cut-glass decanter and glasses gleamed in the subdued lantern light.

The fingers of Malley's left hand rested like nervous stick insects on the brocade cloth surface. 'Well,' he began tentatively, 'we ain't goin' to get far 'til first light, by which time — '

'By which time,' interrupted Quainsley, still pacing, 'the prisoner you were holding — who has so enterprisingly escaped — will be long gone, leaving us with one empty cell and two very full pine coffins.' He halted at the far end of the room and stared at the wall. Not at all satisfactory, is it?'

The judge dragged his watery stare from the decanter, swallowed a threatened belch and settled his hands on his formidable stomach.

'Highly unsatisfactory,' he croaked, 'but not entirely of Malley's doing. He could not possibly have known of the planned killing of Hank Scots; the man had obviously cultivated personal enemies. On the other hand, it is arguable that the fella he had jailed should have been searched more thoroughly and not permitted the luxury of a knife hidden in his shirt by which he was eventually able to overpower the deputy guarding him, kill the poor soul and escape. All that said, however — '

'More than enough, Maitland, more than enough,' said Quainsley, turning from the wall to resume his pacing. 'The facts are blatant enough. We go for weeks, months, with the town going about its business — the money business — in a perfectly straightforward, everyday manner, and then . . . '

He paused mid step, raised an arm and his eyes. 'All this. A more than normally troublesome drunk who turns out to be a desperate killer — who was he, by the way? — and the unexplained murder of my number one security guard. This, my friends, in one day.'

Quainsley strode on defiantly, turned and lunged back to the table, the palms of his hands flat on the brocade. 'Separate and completely unconnected incidents, I ask myself, or are they in some way a part of the same?'

'I cannot see the remotest reason why they should be,' blustered the judge. 'How could they? Why should they?'

'Tell me,' shrugged Quainsley, standing fully upright again, 'tell me I am being overly suspicious, superstitious even — or just too damn smart by half.'

'Well, of course . . . ' blustered McArthur.

'Yuh could be right, 'course yuh could,' said Malley, 'but there ain't a snitch of evidence to say yuh are.'

'Or to say I am not,' grinned Quainsley cynically.

'Yes, yes,' began the judge again, 'but this is all talk. I suggest we cut our losses — sad but a whole sight more practical than raising a posse to go chasing after a man who, if he has any sense, is well clear of the territory and heading for the border even as I speak.'

'Sheriff?' asked Quainsley, peering hard at Malley.

The lawman's fingers tapped quietly for a moment. 'T'ain't in my nature to let a killer go free on my spread. T'ain't the law neither. But right now I got two such scumbags: one gone, one still here in town. So mebbe I should get to concentratin' on the home patch.'

'Or you could, of course, find that your killers are one and the same person,' smiled Quainsley again. 'Have you thought of that possibility?'

'Can't say I have,' grunted Malley, shifting uncomfortably under Quainsley's probing gaze.

'Most unlikely,' huffed the judge. 'Trouble with you, Louis, you're lettin' age niggle at you; getting overcautious, too anxious. You should relax more.'

'Which is your way of saying when am I going to put a hand to that decanter there and pour us all a drink?' grinned Quainsley.

'Well, since you mention it — '

Sheriff Malley's fingers began to tap again. Quainsley might have a point, he pondered. He just might at that.

He came quickly to his feet. 'Not for me,' he grunted. 'Things to do. I'll bid yuh goodnight.'

★   ★   ★

The main street was deserted by the time Sheriff Malley reached the board-walk from the labyrinth of the bank building. Light still burning in one

36

room at the Plainsman, he noted; half a dozen at the Palace; rest of the town was quiet and in darkness, save for Doc Baynam's surgery. Maybe he would look in on the old stick on his way to his office.

'Glad you stopped by,' said Doc, running a hand through the wisps of what remained of his hair. 'Wanted to see yuh, anyhow. Somethin' yuh should know.'

Malley followed the stooped, shuffling physician into his cluttered back room and waited till the old man had primed and lit the lantern before speaking. 'Don't tell me we got more trouble. I've had my share for one day.'

'Well,' murmured Doc, 'depends how yuh get to lookin' at trouble.' He rummaged through a scattering of papers on his rolltop desk. 'Coupla things come up yuh should mebbe know about.' He selected a single sheet of paper. 'Wire came through for me at the rail-head t'night. It's from my opposite number out Narrowcot.'

'Narrowcot?' frowned Malley. 'Heck, that's gettin' for a hundred miles north.'

'I know exactly where it is, Sheriff,' snapped Doc. 'That ain't the point — the point bein' that the Mason gang hit the bank there three days back.'

'So?' frowned Malley again.

'So, it happens my opposite number was treatin' one of the gang badly wounded and left for dead in the raid. Must've been ramblin' some in his fever, but before he finally died he kept repeatin' the phrase: *See yuh in Jackson . . . See yuh in Jackson.* Just that, nothin' more.' Doc blinked and scratched through the wispy drifts of his hair. 'Yuh could be lookin' to a visit from the Mason gang, I reckon. Not to be envied.'

Malley swallowed and began to sweat again. 'Yuh said there were a coupla things.'

'Sure,' said Doc, laying aside the wire. 'Second thing concerns that deputy yuh lost tonight: knife that killed

Hank Scots also killed your man. I can tell. Blades leave their own identity. So I figure that the somebody who murdered Hank rounded off his handiwork for the night by killin' your deputy. In other words, he knew the prisoner and sprung him. And I also figure for the killer still bein' right here in Jackson. Somewhere.'

5

Sixty miles north of the booming, bustling town of Jackson on a morning already thick with heat and flies and the shimmering gleam of baked desert dirt, five men reined their sweat-lathered mounts into the shade of an outcrop of boulders and rested quietly for a while, content to slake their thirsts from warm canteens and wet the muzzles of their horses.

The Mason gang — brothers Duke, Matt and Jacob, Charlie Drace and Zeb Crow — had ridden hard since long before sun-up, and now, with less than five miles to go before they hit the railroad at Hollowneck Junction had reached that moment when choices had to be made, firm decisions taken, their futures shaped up or closed down.

'Well,' said Duke, stoppering his

canteen with a decisive slap, 'we agreed? Nobody fidgetin' round what we already talked through? Say so now or forever hold yuh peace.'

'Count me in,' nodded Matt.

'Same here,' added Jacob, spitting deep into the sand.

Charlie Drace adjusted his hat importantly. 'It's big,' he said flatly. 'Biggest thing we ever done.'

'That's for a fact,' grinned Duke. 'They don't come much bigger. But there comes a time — '

'Yeah, yeah,' drawled Drace, 'I heard yuh say all that business about a fella gettin' his one big chance. Mebbe so. Could also be his last, o'course.'

'That's defeatist talk, Charlie, and yuh know it,' scowled Matt. 'Hell, we been in enough scrapes to name any one of 'em as bein' our last. Just been in one, ain't we? Just lost a decent fella and a good friend back there at Narrowcot. Weren't no big deal for poor Harry, was it? But he weren't complainin'.'

'He sure as hell ain't now!' tittered

Jacob. 'God rest his soul if he's passed on,' he added solemnly.

'We should've gone back for him,' mouthed Zeb Crow from the deep shadow of his broad-brimmed hat. 'I ain't never been for leavin' a shot comrade.'

'All right, all right,' counselled Duke with an edge of impatience, 'don't let's get to some long wranglin' debate. There ain't the time.' He settled his hands on his reins. 'Ain't one of us not pained by what happened to Harry. One of the hazards of ridin' this side of the law. But the fact is, it's over and done. No blame, no recriminations, no goin' back. And no ghosts. Harry would have said the same been any one of us. So, we move on.'

'We do indeed,' nodded Matt, fumbling in his shift for a half-bottle of whiskey.

'That necessary?' snapped Duke.

'Nope,' grinned Matt. 'T'ain't *necessary*, but I sure as hell *like* it, Brother Duke!'

'Yeah, well, yuh go easy, yuh hear?' said Duke. 'Now, let's get to it, shall we? Just remind ourselves of what it is we're supposed to be about. We pulled enough from the bank at Narrowcot to finance the Jackson raid. Fresh mounts, more guns, ammunition, new clothes — fancy cuts, Eastern style — and still enough over to be the men about town 'til we pull the job. Agreed?'

There was a general murmur of agreement.

'Good,' continued Duke, licking at a beading of sweat on his top lip. 'So now we split. I head for the Junction, pick up the train from Denver, be in Jackson day and a half from now. Time enough, I reckon, to take a good look at the situation, get to know the patterns, bank's timetable and put the finishin' touches to my plan.

'You four, meantime, ride for Campsville, make the necessary purchases real quiet, no livin' it up or drawin' attention to yourselves — then yuh ride for Jackson. Yuh take rooms at the

Plainsman. Gus Chappell's our man there. Long-standin' friend, and he owes me. You'll do nothin' then 'til I make contact — and by that time we shall be all set to hit the Western Central and South Peaks bank in the biggest raid this territory's ever seen. Enough to keep us in luxury for the rest of our lives. Yessir!' He smiled, his eyes suddenly bright and alive. 'Yuh got all that? It clear enough for yuh?'

'Clear enough, Brother,' said Jacob. 'You just leave it to us.'

'S'right,' slurred Matt, before belching.

'Bank at Jackson is like a fortress,' announced Crow. 'I seen it once. Guards thick as flies. Goin' to take more than a set of fancy coats and Colts to hit that and live. How yuh plannin' it, or ain't yuh got to that?'

Duke's stare tightened and narrowed. 'Leave the plannin' to me. You just be there, neat, clean and no trouble.'

Drace adjusted his hat again. 'Plan'd better be good, Duke,' he said quietly.

'Sound as a nut, no cracks, no chances. We ain't gone this big before. Could be we're goin' too big.'

'Not so,' said Duke, his smile breaking again. 'I feel this one in my bones; the last job, no more hard ridin', no more hidin'. The Mason gang is goin' to pull out of Jackson to a well-earned retirement.' He slapped his mount's neck. 'So yuh can all get to thinkin' how yuh goin' to spend yuh golden years.'

Drace grunted and murmured something about being grateful enough to get to the end of this year, but no one seemed to be listening.

★   ★   ★

Later, on that same day, as the once weekly train from Denver to Jackson clattered, clanged and steamed its way across the desert towards Hollowneck Junction, Miras Carter, one of a half-dozen passengers in the first-class carriage, contemplated the reach of the afternoon shadows and fancied they reminded him of lawmen.

It was ridiculous, of course; shadows were only shadows, the long sunlit shapes of the rocky outcrops, distant peaks and ranges. But shadows were silent and dark; they could creep up on you, take you by surprise, leave you with no time at all to run from their reach. Same could be said of lawmen.

Not all lawmen, true enough. There were those who fumbled and rumbled around like sick steers; others who had always been shadows. Men like Marshal Doolan. Sam Doolan had been the shadow at Carter's heels for more years than he cared to recall. The Windback Plains, Remo town, Knaresville, Boxton, the Big Knee ranges, and then Denver. Carter would not have reckoned for Doolan making it all those miles to Denver. He had figured for him calling it a day, taking to the rocker, pipe and shaded veranda. Not Doolan. Nossir. Doolan kept coming, reaching like the shadow; one minute there, the next gone — save that you always knew he was never far away and would be back, usually when least expected.

Well, maybe not this time. Maybe this time he really had given the marshal the slip, eased his way out of Denver unheard, unseen, just another passenger on the weekly run to Jackson.

Hell, he thought, shifting in his seat at the dusty window, that had better be the case. Last person he wanted to see in Jackson would be Doolan. The whole venture, every inch of the strategy in the planned raid depended on anonymity; the unknown face that presented itself as trustworthy, honest, and respectable. One word from Doolan would shatter the image on a breath!

But it was not going to happen. No, not this time. There had been too much effort put into the planning, good brains giving of their best: Geraldine Dreyfus, Lawton, Oliver Adams, Red James, the best in the business. And only the best would do in a job this big.

Take Lawton, for an instance. Now he —

The train lurched, shot its white hot sparks in a spitting shower as the bell clanged and brakes were applied.

'Hollowneck Junction . . . Hollowneck,' called the conductor, moving slowly through the carriages. 'Five minutes water stop. Five minutes only. Hollowneck Junction . . .'

Miras Carter waited till the engine had spat, spluttered and ground to a halt before coming to his feet. He would stretch his legs, take a breath of fresh air, light a cigar, relax in the consoling thought of reaching Jackson and Geraldine Dreyfus's bed soon after midnight. The shadows — and Doolan — could go to hell!

It was not until he had stepped through the carriage door to the observation platform that he noticed the lone passenger boarding at the second-class car.

Duke Mason, he frowned, the cigar resting idly and unlit between his fingers, what the hell was a fellow the likes of the leader of the Mason gang doing out here? On the run, dodging the law to stay two steps ahead as ever? Hardly looked in a panic, thought Carter, easing softly into the shade of the carriage roof overhang; in fact, just the opposite, calm as a cat in the sun, broad smile there for the conductor, no hurry, barely breaking sweat.

But out here, in the desert, at a rundown watering-up junction? Where was the rest of the gang? Duke Mason had never travelled as a lone gun. Always had his brothers and his sidekicks to hand. So just why was he heading alone for Jackson? Mason was bad news any place, but right now, in Jackson, at a time like this . . . He would need to keep a careful watch on the fellow.

Three of the five minutes halt at the junction had passed before Carter got to lighting his cigar. He had been otherwise occupied — staring into shadows again.

6

There was still almost an hour to full light when Sheriff Malley, tired-eyed, weary and unshaven, crossed the deserted main street and headed for the Plainsman Hotel.

Doc Baynam's earlier revelations and opinions had done nothing to calm his already strained nerves or induce much needed sleep. Questions — there were far too many of them. Just who and where was the killer with a fancy for blade work? Where was the prisoner Chad Lawton had brought to book, and why had he been sprung from the town jail? And why had Hank Scots been murdered?

In all his years as sheriff of Jackson, Malley had never known a worse time. And the trouble was, he thought on a quiet grunt to himself, he had a nasty, festering suspicion things might get a whole heap more troublesome before they got better, especially if the problems were soon to be compounded by the arrival in town of the Mason gang. What was at the root of their sudden interest in Jackson?

He stepped quickly from the board-walk to the open hotel door and paused a moment, squinting into the dim lantern glow of the musty reception area.

'Yuh there, Gus?' he called, crossing to the desk.

'My, my, ain't you some early bird this mornin',' smiled Gus Chappell, emerging like a shadow from his back-room office. 'What's yuh problem, Sheriff? Can't sleep, or yuh gone and lost another prisoner? Only jokin', o'course.'

'Yuh'd just better be,' rasped Malley on a dry, dusty throat. 'I ain't in no mood for smart talk.' He eased the brim of his hat from his forehead. 'Now, concernin' this fella Oliver Adams yuh got stayin' here, what yuh

51

know of him? He left his room; been about town?'

'Ain't exchanged more than a dozen words with him,' shrugged Gus. 'And I ain't his keeper, and I don't go a deal on nosy spyin', so I wouldn't know to his whereabouts, save that he's sleepin' right now and there ain't nobody sharin' his bed. This is a respectable establishment.'

'Never doubted it, Gus,' said Malley wearily. 'Just checkin', that's all.'

'Sure yuh are, and yuh got good reason for doin' so. Town ain't been a safe place these past hours. Folk get jumpy. Yuh need to get yuh hands on that killer, and fast.' Gus sniffed loudly and adjusted the armbands on his shirt sleeves. 'Chances are, o'course, he ain't around no more. He's mebbe scooted, hit the desert trail. Might be in the hills by now. Yuh raisin' a posse?'

'No, I reckon not. Too damned late for that. And I figure for bein' needed here.'

'Yuh expectin' trouble?' frowned Gus.

'None specific, but after two killin's, well, who's to say?' Malley adjusted his hat again. 'You just keep a close watch, eh? Anythin' that don't figure, yuh tell me; understand? Anythin'.'

'Yuh got it, Sheriff,' grinned Gus. 'Meantime, yuh checked out that fancy woman I hear's stayin' at the Palace? Talk of the town among the menfolk. Must be some looker, eh? Now, if it were me in your boots, I'd be checkin' her out at a pace!'

'Yuh got an evil mind, Gus Chappell,' clipped Malley, turning back to the door. 'But mebbe you're right. Could be I'll be doin' just that — checkin' her out.'

'Best of luck,' winked Gus. 'And yuh gettin' paid for it at that!'

Malley stepped to the boardwalk, took a deep breath of the fresh dawn air, checked his timepiece and decided it was time for coffee. Palace coffee, poured from a silver pot.

He was unaware of the eyes watching him from the window overlooking the street and the soft smile at Oliver Adams's lips.

★ ★ ★

'It's like they say,' said Bertram Carbonne, stifling a deep yawn, 'troubles don't come spread out, do they? Yuh get one, yuh get a whole heap of them, and gettin' bigger by the hour. I know, don't have to tell me, I been there.'

He shivered, flexed his shoulders and gestured to the table for Malley to help himself to the fresh coffee. 'Be my guest — even though it is a mite early.' He watched the sheriff as he supped gratefully at the coffee. 'Don't mind my sayin' so, Frank, but yuh look in need of some long sleep.'

'Say that again,' murmured Malley. He took another sup of the coffee. 'Lawton been quiet through the night?' he asked carefully.

'Well, I ain't been sittin' at his door

54

exactly,' sneered Carbonne, 'so I wouldn't know, and it is hardly a matter of policy at the Palace to get to snoopin' on its valued guests.' The man preened himself importantly for a moment. 'We do have standards, Frank,' he added benevolently.

Malley swallowed the last of his coffee. 'Sure yuh do — but I bet yuh know every damn movement of that good-lookin' woman yuh got in number seventeen!'

Carbonne stiffened, his quick glance registering surprise. 'Well, as it happens,' he said with a nod of modesty, 'I did happen to notice her in our dining-room at around nine last night, making the acquaintance of that fella, Lawton, since you mention him.'

'Well, now,' said Malley, 'ain't he just one helluva fast worker where the ladies are concerned?'

'Oh, I wouldn't say that. Miss Dreyfus is awaiting the arrival of her fiancé from Montana. Due here on the next train in.' Carbonne consulted his timepiece as if for confirmation. 'Midnight tonight. So I wouldn't think — '

'No accountin' to a woman's ways when she gets to facing a charmer like Lawton,' said Malley, crossing the room to the door, pausing for a moment, then turning slowly to add, 'Chad Lawton wear fancy scented water by any chance?'

'Now, how in hell would I know a thing like that?' huffed Carbonne, his eyebrows lifting like crows to flight. 'But as a matter of fact, no, he doesn't. At least he wasn't last night.'

'I'll be back when the lady's had her breakfast,' grunted Malley. 'Meantime, keep watchin', keep lookin' — and stay sniffin'.'

The sheriff had reached the board-walk again to the first glint of the sun in the east when Oliver Adams, still at the street-facing window at the Plainsman, took a large red bandanna from a pocket and flourished it lavishly across his face.

An onlooker might well have taken the gesture for some sort of signal.

* * *

Frank Malley would have been mid street, exposed and a sitting target at that early hour, had Miss Peabody, already busying herself with a besom on the boardwalk fronting her millinery store, not called her 'Good morning, Sheriff', and halted Malley a mere four steps into his stride from the Palace.

The blaze of the first three shots from a Winchester levelled from somewhere on the rooftops opposite kicked the dirt at the sheriff's feet, spinning him back to crash the base of his spine on the boardwalk steps and raise a clouding flurry of dust and dirt as his Colt came instinctively to hand and he blinked madly for a shape.

The fourth shot, ripping across the fading whine and echo of the others, plunged like a white hot shaft into Malley's shoulder, raising a sudden spurt of blood over his shirt and down his arm.

The Colt loosened in his grip. He

rolled, blind now to the street, the rooftops, shapes of emerging bodies as folk eased and edged their ways from cover. He heard Miss Peabody's scream, the clatter of her besom, the thud of her collapse; creaking doors, swinging batwings; shouts, yells, and was tensed for the fatal fifth shot that would end it.

It never came.

The gunman, fearful perhaps of being spotted, suffering a sudden loss of nerve, or maybe under orders, was heard no more that morning — and certainly never seen — as the street began to fill with anxious, curious, scurrying folk.

It was a full five minutes before Doc Baynam was able to elbow his way through the throng to Malley's side. Jake Haston and Bertram Carbonne were already there, Judge Maitland McArthur, still in his vast wrap-around dressing-gown, shouting his orders as if whipping up the energy for the start of a cattle drive.

Benjamin Bright had opened his store for the 'walking wounded' should there be any; Polly Sweet was ministering to Miss Peabody, a clutch of girls from the gaming house hovering in the shadows, and Louis Quainsley ordering the woman in his bed to 'get some clothes on, f'Cris'sake!'

Geraldine Dreyfus had stirred between the sheets in her bed, a satisfied smile breaking slowly across her face, and risen at her leisure. She could see no reason to hurry to be an onlooker at a scene she had pictured many times. The sheriff, she imagined, would be dead by now, anyway.

Chad Lawton was dressing hurriedly, and fumbling through every movement, at the same time cursing his misfortune at occupying a back room at the Palace. Gus Chappell had seen all he wanted to see and retreated to his office, locked the door, closed the drapes and opened his only bottle of decent whiskey.

Oliver Adams was one of the few people not watching events. He had left the window overlooking the street, his back twitching under a cold, clinging chill. It was a nervous reaction he was prone to when things began to go wrong.

7

'Winchester — there's the clue, damn it!' winced Sheriff Malley under the probing touch of Doc Baynam. 'Tell from the roar of it. A quality piece — and I seen only one such rifle recently. Fella I had jailed had it, took it when he was sprung and plans, it seems, to keep right on usin' it.' He winced again. 'Easy there, Doc, will yuh?'

'Ain't no easy way round this, Frank,' murmured Doc, peering closer at Malley's shoulder wound. 'Nasty mess yuh got here. Deep, and I figure for the lead still bein' buried. Gonna have to put yuh to the knife.'

Louis Quainsley paced carefully round Bertram Carbonne's private room at the Palace hotel before pausing to stare thoughtfully at the door. 'So this gunman — this rag-bag drifter — is still in town, or close by. That what yuh sayin', Sheriff?' he said, turning slowly. 'A madman on the loose.'

'Just that,' coughed Judge Maitland McArthur, wheezing on a glowing cigar. 'Stark ravin' insane.'

'Probably,' croaked Malley. 'But I don't figure why he's takin' the risk. Damn it, I never clapped eyes on him 'til a few hours back. So what's the big beef?'

'He just don't like yuh,' said Carbonne, brushing at a speck of dust on the lapel of his coat. 'Revenge. A twisted mind. You name it, he's got it. More to the point, what we goin' to do about him? Can't just leave him to roam free. No sayin' who might be next in his sights.'

'I'll have my guards mount a search,' snapped Quainsley. 'They won't leave a stone unturned. Every home, every business, even the bank, they'll all be gone over, room by room, inch by inch.' He huffed and stiffened as if to display his authority. 'Meantime, I'll wire

Denver for more lawmen. A dozen; two if necessary. We'll close the town down, tight as a nut, 'til the sonofabitch killer is swingin' at the end of a rope.'

'All a mite drastic, aint it?' said Doc, still concentrating on the sheriff's wound. 'Hell, the scumbag ain't no more than a drunk drifter, is he? Probably cleared town an hour back. Closin' down the town ain't goin' — '

'And what about the other killin's?' chipped Quainsley. 'Hank Scots, Sheriff's deputy . . . what about them? Is our Winchester man also handy with a knife? Or do we have two killers on the loose? First consideration is the town and keepin' it secure — against all-comers. Ain't that so, Mr Malley?'

Malley glanced quickly at Doc Baynam, catching his eye in the same thought of the Mason gang rumour. 'Well,' he began slowly, 'that's gotta be right, o'course, but bringin' in a whole army of men — '

'Louis here is right,' interrupted Judge McArthur on another wheeze.

'Can't leave things to chance, and with you out of the reckonin' for the time bein', Frank, we need help to play safe.' He blew a thick cloud of smoke. 'I'm for wirin' Denver. This mornin'. Right now.'

'We got spare rooms here,' offered Carbonne quickly. 'Costs could be cut accordingly.'

Quainsley shot the man a withering look. 'You bet the costs will be cut,' he snapped. 'To the bone! This is an emergency, Bertram, a state of civic priority. And don't you go forgettin' it.' He straightened his frock coat dramatically and crossed to the table to collect his hat. 'I'll get things organized immediately. Time's pressin'.'

Quainsley had reached the door when he paused and turned again. 'Most attractive young woman you have stayin' here, Bertram. You must introduce me sometime. Tell her to join me in the bar for drinks at noon.'

'But she ain't — ' began Carbonne to Quainsley's disappearing back as

64

Malley winced again, Doc grunted and McArthur blew more smoke.

★ ★ ★

Gus Chappell stared at the half-empty bottle of his best whiskey and decided, on a long belch and a dazed haze of swimming images, that he had maybe had enough for now. There was always another day, another night, another crisis.

You could bet on the crisis for sure, he thought, slumping back in his chair in the back room at the Plainsman. Something would come up, somebody would start something — already had, damn it. Crazed gunman downing the sheriff like that; some madman stalking the town with a deadly blade. Hell, Jackson had gone sourmash loopy!

He belched again, closed his eyes and figured he might doze a while, sleep off the worst of the best whiskey. Damn it, he grinned, how could you have the worst of the best. Made no sense . . .

And Gus Chappell might well have drifted into a confused, deep sleep had a door somewhere above him not been opened and closed, a floorboard creak and footsteps sound hurriedly along the corridor to the stairs.

Oliver Adams on the move, thought Gus, coming fully awake with a start. Odd time to take the air, though, only minutes after a street shooting and half the town spooked near out of its skin. Fellow could get his head blown off taking such a risk. Maybe he should go tell him, warn him.

But the gloomy, unlit reception area was deserted and Adams, already halfway down the street by the time Gus had made it unsteadily to his feet and located the door in his office.

'Hell,' he mouthed, wiping his fingers across his eyes, time had obviously come for a wash, a tall pot of strong coffee, even a change of shirt, if he had one . . . But maybe not before he had taken the spare key and put his head round the door of the room Oliver

Adams was so covetously occupying.

Just what in the name of tomorrow had a slick-dressed, spats and polished leather-booted fellow got to hide in a place like Jackson? More intriguingly, why was he staying at the Plainsman?

It took Gus a full five minutes to make it up the stairs and along the corridor to the door of Adams's room. This was not, of course, he reminded himself, the sort of thing he would do normally — at least not often, and then only when he deemed it necessary in the interests of the business. This was just such an instance, he figured, not sure of quite why it was.

The drapes had been closed against the first shafts of sunlight, settling the room in a dappled glow where the deeper shadows lurked in the corners like sleeping bodies. Gus waited, the door still partly open at his back, blinked to adjust his hazy vision and peered over the room's new contents.

Adams's valise there, far end of the bed, clean shirts laid out, another set of spats, pair of expensive boots, two or three silk bandannas, face towel and bottles of what might be medicines (could be the fellow had a roustabout stomach), or could be scented waters. At least one was scented water, he decided, sniffing to catch the lingering odour.

He checked out the belongings again to be certain he could list them to Sheriff Malley and had turned to slip back to the corridor when the stain, dark but not ancient, caught his eye.

Well, he pondered, squatting to peer closer, he might not be the keenest when it came to keeping the place smart, but he knew every darned stain, floor to ceiling, in every room — and this, right here on the carpet, was new, no more than hours old.

He touched it, ran his fingers over it, lifted them to his nose, sniffed. Two jacks to the joker this was dried blood. Whose blood? Adams's? Had to be. So how come the fellow had got to cutting himself to drip this much blood? If it was not such a fool-headed thought he would have reckoned for him having been in some sort of fight.

'Hell,' murmured Gus behind another belch, he would get to cleaning up when Adams had left. Meantime, it just went on the list of things to tell Malley, assuming he had the slightest interest.

★ ★ ★

At about the same time on that same morning, as the sun came up full and bright and promising a hot day by noon, the Mason gang, minus their leader, rode into the desert-dirt town of Campsville.

Few folk at that hour gave them more than a cursory glance. Drifters, they would have thought, types the town was a second home to on the busy trail through to the high life in Jackson. They would rest up a day or so, spend some money (saving most of it for the gaming and girls at Jackson) eat cheap, drink still cheaper, and pull out. The folk of

Campsville had seen it all before, any number of times. It all went with the territory and the time of year.

Even so, there was just the hint of a prickling in Sheriff Ben Moore's neck as he watched the four riders hitch their mounts at the Fast Dollar saloon. At least one of the men he had seen before, some place up north at about the time the bank at Draycott had been hit.

Some while back, of course, and he could easily be mistaken.

8

You could say what you liked about Sheriff Moore being the lone-hand law in a two-bit dirt trail town — the poor, patched-pants relation of prosperous Jackson — but you would have to give it to him for diligence.

Ben Moore took wearing the star in Campsville as serious business; law was the law, he reckoned, wherever you upheld it. Campsville was no different to anywhere else and therefore, he maintained, 'You do your best by it, keep your eyes skinned and your memory buttermilk fresh'.

And so it was that within an hour of the arrival in town of the four members of the Mason gang, he had put a name to the face of Charlie Drace and unearthed an old poster proving that Drace had indeed been involved in the bank raid at Draycott some five years back and was still carrying a price on his head.

'Ridin' along of Will Slater and his boys in them days,' he had told his deputy, 'but I heard say as how he split soon after Draycott. So who's he with now, why's he here, and where's he headin'? Don't recognize his companions, at least not yet; if he's headin' for Jackson, and that's for a near certainty, then he's only passin' through Campsville. Fact is, though, there's still a price on his head and he's still a wanted man.'

'So we bring him in?' the deputy had asked.

'Not yet. Not 'til I've had a while to check on them fellas he's ridin' with. Yuh know what they say, snakes bask along of snakes. We might be for baggin' all four . . .'

★ ★ ★

And Sheriff Ben Moore, the committed, diligent, lone-hand law in Campsville,

72

might very well have bagged a haul, and thus ended the reign of the Mason gang, had Matt Mason's reserve supply of whiskey (the bottle kept buried in his shirt) not run dry and his ever-roving eye not alighted on the Fast Dollar saloon's local beauty, Daisy-May Fortune.

His brother, Jacob, along with Charlie Drace and Zeb Crow had urged that they go easy at the saloon.

'A few beers, settle the dust, then we get to the business of the supplies. No messin' and real peaceful,' Jacob had ordered once their mounts had been hitched, but probably on the deaf ears of Matt who, even then with the whiskey supplies in sight, had already caught a glimpse over the batwings of the intriguing Daisy-May.

The pattern of events took shape in under the hour.

Jacob, Drace and Crow drank beer, Matt falling quickly, hungrily to the whiskey, every measure from the fast diminishing bottle relished on the view of Daisy-May languishing provocatively among the gathering of a handful of girls at the end of the bar.

The only other customer presence in the saloon that morning were the two men seated at a table in the corner; quiet fellows, deep in conversation, minding their own business.

At least, that was how it seemed and should have stayed, and did until the younger man of the seated pair came to his feet and crossed to the group of girls. It was at this moment that Matt Mason gulped deep and noisily on a freshly poured measure, stiffened and glared long and hard at the young man's approach and particular interest in Daisy-May.

'Lady there's already spoken for,' drawled Matt, replacing his glass on the bar with a deliberate gesture.

'That so, ma'am?' asked the man, tipping the brim of his hat to the woman.

Daisy-May merely shrugged, eased her shape to one hip and lowered her eyes.

'Seems like an open range to me, mister,' smiled the man.

Matt Mason sighed and poured another measure from the bottle.

'Leave it, will yuh?' hissed Crow from the corner of his mouth.

'You do just that, yuh hear?' added Drace, turning his back on the girls. 'This ain't the time — it ain't the place. You'll get to all the girls yuh want in Jackson.'

Matt studied the measure, fingered the glass, raised it and sank the drink in one. 'Yuh heard me first time, fella,' he sneered, turning to face the man. 'I said the lady's spoken for. She still is; ain't nothin' changed, so mebbe you'll just stand aside there, get back to yuh friend, eh? I'll tell yuh when there's one of these ladies free for your attention, though frankly yuh don't look nowhere near old enough to me to get to indulgin' in such manly affairs.'

The colour rose in the man's cheeks. His eyes brightened. A line of sweat beaded across his brow.

'We said to leave it,' growled Drace.

'This ain't no business of yours, Charlie,' mouthed Matt. 'Be obliged if yuh'd keep out of it.'

'Yuh booze-brained fool, don't yuh never . . . ' Drace had begun again, only to hear the words grating in his throat, his mouth dry to dirt, a cold, skimming iciness settle across his spine as he watched the young man reach for his Colt, draw it in a flash of his hand and probably even then believe he was those vital seconds ahead of Matt Mason's retaliation.

Not so.

The man's Colt blazed sure enough, once, twice, but the aim from the hip was unsteady, nervy and already shifting on the second shot as Mason's gun roared its answer in a blaze that threw the man back in a twisted heap of limbs and flying blood.

'Yuh sonofa-goddamn-bitch!' cursed Drace.

Zeb Crow fell back against a chair; Jacob Mason spun away instinctively, his thoughts already working on the reaction in the street beyond the bar.

The girls huddled together like suddenly bedraggled blooms, Daisy-May doing her best to herd them to the cover of the bar where the potman crouched, his eyes closed, hands clamped to his ears.

The dead man's partner, an older, slower-moving man, had come to his feet at the table at the first shot, his face grey with fear, body shuddering, legs weakening as he pushed back his chair, turned and stumbled towards the 'wings.

Matt Mason's Colt blazed again, this time on a tittered burst of giggling, a crash of the whiskey bottle to the floor, Charlie Drace's growls and curses, all to no avail in the roar that buried lead in the stumbling man's back, clean between the shoulder-blades, and brought him slithering to a twitching halt, one half of him reaching across the shadowed boardwalk.

'Crazy-headed fool!' yelled Jacob.

'What yuh gone and done?'

'Damned if I don't get to shootin' you like a mad dog one of these days, Matt-bloody-Mason,' scowled Zeb Crow.

'Get the hell out!' shouted Drace, pushing Matt ahead of him. 'Get to the horses! Ride, damn it!'

The four men were mounted up and swinging their bucking, snorting horses away from the saloon, when Sheriff Moore and his deputy staggered into the sunlit dirt, clear in the path of the racing mounts.

'Stand aside there, yuh fools,' bellowed Drace.

The deputy made to level his Winchester, but managed no more than a futile gesture under a wild blaze from Matt Mason's Colt that killed him instantly.

Sheriff Moore fell across the dead body, blood pouring freely from both legs.

It was a full five minutes before the throb of pounding hoofs finally faded from the stunned, bewildered town of

Campsville and were lost somewhere on the trail heading south.

★　★　★

At shortly after noon on that day, with Ben Moore confined to his bed under the watchful if slightly boozed gaze of the town's ageing doctor, newly sworn-in deputy, Lou Winters, waited anxiously for the sheriff to complete the handwritten notes he was to deliver to Jackson.

'Shouldn't be strainin' yourself like this, Ben,' frowned the doc from the side of the bed. 'Damn it, you're lucky to be alive, and you've lost enough blood from those leg wounds to darn near fill a pail. I'm tellin' yuh, fella — '

'I know exactly what yuh tellin' me, Doc. Yuh been doin' it for the last two hours, and I'm obliged for your concern,' croaked the sheriff, shuffling the papers in front of him, 'but we got a crisis here, bad as a crisis comes. Them scumbags we just had rattlin' all hell through here this mornin' were no less than the Mason gang, or at least four of the rats. That's for a fact. Found some old posters, didn't I?' He screwed his eyes at a sudden stab of pain. 'Now I don't figure for me makin' no wild guesses when I say I reckon for them headin' straight for Jackson. Right?'

'I'd say so,' nodded Doc.

'Lou?' asked the sheriff.

'Gotta be,' agreed the deputy, turning his hat self-consciously through his fingers where he waited at the door to the bedroom. 'Headed due south, didn't they? Only one place that trail's leadin'.'

'Right,' said Ben, 'so that's where we — leastways the law — bring the sonsof-murderin'-bitches to book. Jail 'em, then hang 'em on a long drop!' He winced, groaned and gathered his senses. 'I written it all here, every last detail of what happened today in our town. No point in whippin' ourselves over it, what's done is done. Now we gotta do our best by the three who died here. Too damned right we have!'

Ben stared hard at Lou Winters. 'Yuh get yourself a fast horse, Lou, best there is and yuh ride hard for Jackson. Take the Water Creek route and stay clear of the main trail. When yuh hit Jackson, yuh go straight to Sheriff Malley. Nobody else, yuh hear? Yuh give him my notes. He'll know how to handle things. And then yuh shift yuh butt back here fast as yuh can. Got it?'

'Got it, boss,' said Lou, stepping forward to take the notes.

'And now,' began Doc again, 'let's get to puttin' yuh to rights.'

'No, Doc,' said Ben, slumping back on his pillows, his eyes closing. 'Not just yet. Let's open that bottle I got put away in the cabinet there. We're goin' to drink a toast: to the law and to wherever it's waitin' to hit back. Yessir, the law!' He opened one eye. 'And then Lou rides like the wind for Jackson.'

9

Chad Lawton fidgeted uneasily in the quiet corner of the bar at the Silver Palace Hotel, careful not to miss the slightest movement among the few early day drinkers or any of the snatches of conversation drifting between the subdued voices.

'I ain't seen nothin' like it in a lifetime . . .'

'Malley's gotta be the luckiest man alive . . .'

'I heard say the killer's plannin' on a dozen more bodies to satisfy his blood lust . . .'

'Close talk has it he's demandin' five women and ten thousand dollars to leave town . . .'

'Is it true as how they've sent for the army?'

'I'm tellin' yuh, we ain't seen the last of this, or that madman . . .'

Lawton half-smiled to himself, but was still conscious of the sweat in his neck. It was not like Red James to foul up a shooting; nor did it seem believable that for the first time in his meticulously measured career Oliver Adams's timetable was slipping out of control.

The harsh facts spoke for themselves: Sheriff Malley was still very much alive; the bank's security guards were on a short-fuse alert and moving fast through the town in their search for the mystery killer. It might only be a matter of time before Red was discovered, unless, of course, he had already pulled out. But to where?

Lawton shifted again, this time to acknowledge the quick glance from Geraldine Dreyfus as she passed through the bar to the dining-room on the arm of Louis Quainsley.

Hell, thought Lawton, tapping a finger on the bar, she was running her luck and audacity to the brim.

Time to move, he decided, to break

the rules, go find Adams, learn what had happened to Red, what the next move was going to be. He looked anxiously at his timepiece; still hours to go before the train steaming south carrying Miras Carter reached Jackson.

He grunted. So what would Carter do were he here, he wondered? One thing was for certain, he would not waste his time sitting alone in a quiet corner of some hotel bar figuring what to do.

Chad Lawton had left the Palace and reached the boardwalk to the busy morning street too late to notice the hurrying shape of Gus Chappell heading for the sheriff's office.

* * *

'I'm tellin' yuh, there's no mistake — that was a bloodstain and it weren't there three days back. Now, if yuh ask me — '

Sheriff Malley cleared his throat loudly, shuffled the papers on his desk and glanced quickly at Doc Baynam before making a gesture with his good arm to silence Gus Chappell.

'I'm hearin' yuh, Gus,' he said, stifling a wince. 'Yuh done well. Sounds to me as if Mr Oliver Adams might have some explainin' to do.'

'And this smell,' added Doc, 'the scented water. Yuh sure about that?'

'Sure as I'm standin' here,' nodded Gus. 'Don't get a lot of that sorta thing at the Plainsman. It important?'

'Might be,' said Malley, easing back in his chair. 'Meantime, you keep an eye on the fella. What he does, where he is — '

'Yuh goin' to deputize me?' asked Gus, gripping the lapels of his frock coat.

'Deputize yuh?' frowned Malley. 'Well now, I hadn't exactly figured — '

'Seems to me you're a mite short-handed here, losin' yuh deputies like that. Can't claim, o'course, to be some fast-shootin', hell-for-leather kid, but I can handle a piece; I know the town and the folk in it. All very well Quainsley turnin' his guards loose like he has, but mebbe a softer approach might be just as useful. And I ain't exactly run off my feet at the Plainsman.'

'He's got a point,' said Doc, crossing the office to the window. 'We need another pair of eyes on the town. Gus here might be just the man.'

Malley grunted, fingering the bandage at his shoulder. 'You're right, both of yuh. If yuh want the job — and on a temporary basis if it suits — yuh got it. Can't deny I could do with the help, and I ain't over-keen on takin' on outsiders. Job's yours, Gus. And I'm obliged.'

'Right,' smiled Gus, rubbing his hands. 'So let's get to it, eh? What's yuh priority?'

'Simple enough,' sighed Malley. 'We got a killer on the loose and I want him found. Fast. Any way we can, by any means. And while we're keepin' our eyes peeled on that front, yuh might keep an ear open for any word of the Mason gang hereabouts. They pulled a job at Narrowcot and might be headin' this way.'

The light in the sheriff's office was too dim, too shadow-filled for either Malley or Doc Baynam to see the suddenly pale, drawn look cloud Gus Chappell's face, or to spot the line of sweat break across his brow.

★ ★ ★

'He's a lucky fella, Miss Dreyfus, if you don't mind my saying so. Yessir, your fiancé is very lucky.' Louis Quainsley bowed his head to the woman facing him and watched her carefully, if mischievously, as she returned his slow smile. 'And don't tell me he isn't aware of it,' he added. 'Be a fool if he wasn't, my dear. A real fool.' He waited a moment, his gaze on the glass he fingered absently. 'Do I know him by any chance? I have travelled widely and there aren't many engaged in the business of money I don't know.'

Geraldine Dreyfus was smart enough and had been around long enough not to see the question for what it was — a pointedly timed and prepared probe. 'I doubt it, Mr Quainsley,' she replied softly. 'He tends to operate very discreetly.'

'Discreetly — well, there's an interesting description, one not often heard these days and especially through this territory. Most interesting. Tell me, your Mr . . . I don't think I caught his name.'

'I didn't give it, Mr Quainsley,' said the woman to a tight glare. 'You will be meeting him in a business sense soon enough.'

'Good,' smiled Quainsley. 'I look forward to it. Are we talking business of a . . . financial nature?'

Geraldine Dreyfus sipped delicately at her drink. 'Most definitely, I should think. My fiancé has long been an admirer of the Western Central and South Peaks bank. A first-class operation, he has always said. One never to be overlooked — financially speaking.'

'Really?' glowed Quainsley. 'How gratifying to hear such an opinion. Yes, well, as I say, I shall look forward to our meeting. In the meantime, by way of something of a personal apology for the, shall I say, decidedly unsavoury atmosphere of the town in which you find yourself at the moment — not a usual state, I assure you — I wonder if you would do me the honour of dining with me tonight? Shall we say eight-o'clock, my private quarters at the bank? So much safer in the circumstances, you understand.'

Perfect, thought Geraldine Dreyfus, smiling her acceptance.

The last time a woman had accepted an invitation to a private dinner that readily, she had been intent on robbing me, pondered Louis Quainsley, without dismissing his suspicious musings entirely.

10

It had taken Chad Lawton almost an hour to finally track down Oliver Adams to the shadowed alley at the back of Polly Sweet's gaming house — barely a spit, as it happened, from where the dead body of Hank Scots had been discovered.

'What the hell yuh doin' here?' he hissed, stepping into the deeper shadows. 'Been lookin' all over town for yuh.'

'Tactics, preparation, Mr Lawton,' grinned the round, moon-faced man, his beady eyes twinkling.

'Sight more than tactics needed right now,' snapped Lawton, pulling Adams closer to him so that the words crackled in his ear-drum. 'What happened back there, f'Cris'sake? Red missed. Sheriff's still alive. Things ain't goin' to plan. So where's Red now, and what yuh plannin' next? Yuh know what Carter is for stickin' to the plan.'

Adams eased himself clear of Lawton's grip, dusted the lapels of his frock coat disdainfully, adjusted his cravat again and narrowed his gaze to tight slits. 'Don't do that again, Mr Lawton,' he said bitingly. 'Last man who tried it . . . ' He nodded to the patch where Scots had been found. 'We'll say no more. As for Red, he's out of town for the time being. Somewhere in hiding off the main trail. He'll be back tonight. When it comes to the sheriff, well, shall we say a minor hitch? Nothing we can't handle. Leave the matter with me. You go back to scouting out that bank as you're supposed to be doing.' He paused a moment. 'Miss Dreyfus made contact?' he asked.

'I seen her with Quainsley,' said Lawton.

'Good. She can be trusted to do a thorough job. Meantime — '

'Meantime, I want to hear more about these preparations,' hissed Lawton again.

'What yuh got in mind?'

'A mere entertainment,' shrugged Adams with a flickering grin. 'Something to keep the town occupied, shall we say? You must wait, be patient.'

'Bank guards are turnin' the town over. Yuh'd best watch your back. And go easy with that blade. We've had enough of that for now.'

'My blade, as you call it, and I are inseparable. Bear it in mind. The bank guards are fools. They'll find nothing. Nothing to find, is there? Let's keep it that way. Not too long now before Carter's in town and we make the final move. Don't foul it up.'

★ ★ ★

The four riders lifting the trail dirt to a swirling cloud had held to the same pace in a direct line south for over an hour.

And wisely so, thought Charlie Drace, riding tight behind the lathered mount of Matt Mason. There might not be much chance of the sheriff at Campsville raising a posse to give chase to the hell-raisers who had struck his town, but that was no reason for not putting the place and the events firmly behind them.

He spat viciously over the wind. Damn the whiskey-soaked, mule-headed fool slumped loose-limbed in the saddle ahead of him. Matt Mason was not to be trusted and fast becoming a liability in any planned raid on the bank at Jackson — particularly in a raid so audacious on a bank that size. Hell, one wrong move from the soak, a split second of the booze-bettering judgement, and they could all be figuring in a pine box display at the Boot Hill end of the street.

It might yet come to drastic measures, he mused. And why not, damn it? They had lost a good man in the Narrowcot raid; this was no time to go making a habit of it. There was too much at stake, not least his own life.

'Rest up at the rocks there,' yelled

Jacob above the pounding hoofs, the creaking leather, jangling tack.

'And not before time,' mouthed Zeb Crow, groaning at the soreness in his limbs, the aches seeping into his fingers. Should never have come to this, he thought, it was just not in the planning. And what about the fresh mounts, guns, clothes they were supposed to have organized? What was Duke going to say about that? Would he call off the whole venture? Hell, all a waste of time because of a tonsil-varnished, two-bit drunk . . .

'Yuh got a mighty lot of explainin' to do, Matt Mason,' growled Drace when the four riders were reined up in the cooler, quieter shade of the rocks. 'And yuh can start by tellin' me how it is — '

'Ain't no goin' back,' snapped Jacob on a crack of his reins. 'What's done is done. Shouldn't have been, but there we are.'

Zeb Crow spat angrily. 'That all yuh got to say for that hell-stinkin' mess we left behind back there? *What's done is done* — that it, when we've just scuppered the whole darned plan? Well, I ain't takin' it that easy. Not no how.'

'So what yuh sayin'?' drawled Matt, his eyes still rolling drunkenly. 'Yuh for pullin' out, Zeb? That what yuh tellin' us?'

'I'm for tellin' *you* to pull out,' flared Crow, spitting again. 'Sure I am. Duke'd say the same.'

'Yuh ain't speakin' there for Duke,' clipped Jacob.

'Mebbe he ain't,' said Drace, shifting to the roll of his mount's flanks, 'but he's sure as hell speakin' for me. I figure the same as Zeb — plan's blown, ain't it? How we goin' to ride into Jackson way we're lookin' now, start buyin' fancy coats, guns, horses and all them trappin's, and not raise some eyebrows, eh? You tell me that.'

'Mebbe we don't need to go to all that bother,' shrugged Jacob. 'Hell, all we're doin' is robbin' a bank, f'Cris'sake.'

'So now yuh sayin' we go against

Duke's orders, are yuh?' sniffed Drace. 'Forget all he said and just go our own sweet way, and all because yuh sonofabitch brother here's lost his head to a bottle of booze.'

'Who yuh callin' a sonofabitch?' slurred Matt.

'All right,' shouted Crow, 'let's cool it, shall we? Ain't nothin' useful comin' of talk like this. Ain't gettin' us no place. Question we gotta face is — '

'Who in the name of hell is slippin' about in them rocks up there? That's the question,' said Drace, his eyes narrowing suddenly against the glare to squint at the jagged sprawl of rocks above him. 'And yuh might add to that: how long's he been there, and how much has he heard?'

★ ★ ★

The four men glanced anxiously, furtively at each other, leaving it to Drace, with the clearest view of the reach of rocks, to keep his gaze

96

narrowed and probing.

'Stay talkin' among yourselves,' murmured Drace. 'Dismount. Easy does it. Guide the horses into the deeper shade, force whoever's up there to shift. Leave the rest to me.'

'Yuh goin' after him?' croaked Jacob.

'I sure as hell ain't leavin' him up there,' drawled Drace, slipping from the saddle to the hot, dusty dirt. No sayin' how much the fella's heard, or where he might be figurin' on takin' it. We're goin' to have to make sure he stays put, ain't we? Permanently.'

'Need some help?' offered Crow.

'Just give me some back-up if the lead gets hectic. Otherwise stay outa the fella's sights. Angle he's at, he could pick you off like flies.'

Drace waited, brushed at a pestering fly, tapped the butt of his holstered Colt, nodded to the others and slipped away.

He stayed tight to the shade where he was able to climb, a few steps at a time, then pause, watch, listen, hopeful that

97

the fella was all set to shift to keep the riders in view and remain within earshot of their talk.

Real question to be asked, he thought, wiping the sweat from his eyes as he caught his breath, was, what was a lone fellow doing out here, anyway? He was certainly in no hurry to be anywhere in particular, but how come he was holed-up here in a straggling outcrop of rocks? Only good reason Drace could fathom was to stay out of sight. But that raised a whole raft of other questions . . .

Drace tapped the Colt again and squinted into the glare across the smooth rock faces. The fellow hidden there was staying silent, probably not moving so much as a muscle. Had he seen Drace, spotted that there were now only three riders in the shade? He could maybe afford to sit this out for as long as it took; he was in no hurry, it seemed.

But Drace was. You bet, he thought, moving on through the rocks. There was still no saying what the sheriff back in Campsville might decide on: raising a posse under a newly sworn-in deputy, or maybe getting word down the trail to Jackson on the assumption the hell-raisers were headed that way?

Word down the trail would be the wisest move — which meant an early arrival in Jackson was a priority for the Mason gang if they were to be anything like prepared for putting Duke's plan for the bank raid into action. Always assuming there was still going to be a raid.

Only the nosy fellow here in the rocks was pestering worse than the flies . . .

Drace grunted quietly and moved on slowly, softly, his fingertip grips firm and sure, his steps easy but solid. Nothing to be gained in rushing this, he reckoned. One wrong move, too much noise, a loose rock dislodged, even a pebble clattering unnaturally, would be all it needed for a barrel to appear, stay steady and blast him into oblivion.

Drace climbed on, still hugging the

shade where it plunged and sprawled across the rocks to his right, conscious now of coming ever closer to where he had first seen the man. The sharp prickle of sweat in his neck, tingling over the shorter hairs in the nape, warned of his concentration and not least the fear that there might already be eyes watching every movement, just waiting for that one fatal moment —

'I figure yuh done all the sweatin' yuh need for one day, mister.'

The voice cracked almost jokingly at Drace's back; a slow, easy drawl he recognized without needing to turn to the man. 'Red James?' he croaked, his hands lifting well clear of his gunbelt. 'I ain't mistaken, am I? The same Red James operates out of Denver? My, my. Mite off yuh territory, ain't yuh? And since when has the all-time Red James got to skulkin' back of no man's land?'

'I took yuh measure, Drace, you and the scum you're ridin' with: Zeb Crow and the Masons,' drawled James, the click of the hammer on a drawn Colt echoing eerily. 'What yuh done with Duke? Yuh dumped him, or you boys got somethin' planned?'

'Might ask somethin' similar of yourself,' said Drace, beginning to turn, arms wide, hands still clear. 'Only one thing I could figure for appealin' to the likes of you, Red, 'specially this far out of Denver, is money, plenty of it; sort of 'plenty' you might find in a bank like the one down the trail there in Jackson. Would I be even spittin' distance right?'

A grin broke through the sweat on James's tanned, leathery face. 'Great minds . . . as they say. You and the boys wouldn't be harbourin' the same unwholesome thoughts by any chance, would yuh?'

'Well, now,' shrugged Drace, watching James's gaze tighten under a deepening frown, 'wouldn't that be somethin' of a godalmighty coincidence? Why, if I hadn't heard it from yuh own lips, I'd have figured — '

There was no more figuring to be said or heard in the rocks on that glare-filled day as Charlie Drace's hand flashed like a shimmer of the sunlight to his Colt and had the weapon drawn, levelled and blazing while James still stared, frowning through the possibilities of the amazing coincidence of a double-planned bank raid.

The shots, four in rapid succession across a point-blank distance, were ripping into James even as his trigger finger came to pressure and his single wild shot roared high over Drace's head.

A resting hawk clattered into life as Red James groaned, began to double, his Colt hanging loose and useless in his fingers, his eyes rolling crazily for a last mocking sight of his killer.

'Lost yuh edge there for a minute, Red,' cracked Drace, standing back, his weight slung to one hip. 'Careless. Comes with age, eh? Or is it the greed gettin' to yuh? Still, more for us, Red, more for us. I'll spend your share of the money we'll be liftin' out of Jackson with a thought for you in every bottle I open. And that's a promise!'

11

Miras Carter shrugged off the temptation to nod and doze to the momentum of the speeding locomotive, blinked his eyes wide open and consulted his timepiece once again. Another hour had passed. Three more, if all went well, to their arrival in Jackson. They would seem like days.

He grunted, pocketed the timepiece, leaned closer to the first-class carriage window and peered into the darkness of the deepening night. Little enough to be seen now; distant mountain shapes in a curtain of purple haze; a high starlit sky, moon flat as a watchful eye; the shadows gathering, thickening . . .

Say that again, thought Carter, relaxing into the depths of his seat, Duke Mason being the worst of them. And still raising the same questions, damn him!

Why was the gang leader travelling

alone; why had he boarded at Hollow-neck; what did he have planned in Jackson?

He grunted again and shifted uncomfortably. There was already too much to occupy his thoughts without the clutter of Mason and his roughneck riders who had never been known for either their subtlety or deft approach. Their bodies cluttering the boardwalks of Jackson was something he would not be relishing.

He muttered angrily to himself, glanced at the window again, saw nothing save his own reflection and for some inexplicable but alarming reason, the blurred, drifting image of Marshal Doolan.

'Damn!' he croaked, to the clattering clang and hiss of the night train into Jackson.

* * *

Gus Chappell had changed his shirt — been forced to, and nearly a full week ahead of schedule at that. There had been no choice; all that sweat, till he was near sodden through.

And he was still sweating, damn it, even now, here in the evening cool of his back room, when he would normally be relaxed, taking it easy, reckoning on an early whiskey, maybe contemplating a quiet stroll down to Polly Sweet's place before midnight.

But not tonight. Hell, no, not if there was the slightest chance of the Mason gang hitting town.

He came to his feet from the chair at the table, crossed to the door — left an inch or so ajar for his own satisfaction — squinted one-eyed into the hotel's gloomy reception area where only a single lantern burned fitfully at the end of the desk, eased the door open another inch and glanced anxiously to the lights of the boardwalk. All quiet, no one about, town seemed normal enough, or maybe just too darned spooked after the killings and shooting to come alive.

They would sure as hell be feeling spooked enough once Duke Mason rode in. Gus twitched nervously at the thought. And where would the gun-slinging gang boss head first? Why here, of course, straight to the Plainsman; no hesitation.

'Gus,' he would say, with that half grin curling round his lips like a snake, 'been a while, ain't it? Not since Morrow Town, eh? You remember Morrow Town, don't yuh? Tuesday, fifteenth of August, four years back. Day my boys hit the North Rock Bank. Bad business that, 'specially when yuh get to figurin' somebody must've tipped off the law we were ridin' in. Shame. Now just who could have been that mean, do you suppose? Still, all blown dust now, ain't it, Gus? Sure, it is. Now, when was it you left Morrow Town . . . ?'

And before his next blink, Gus would be agreeing to whatever Duke Mason asked of him. No question, he would have to if he wanted to stay breathing. Gus Chappell had sold out the Mason gang four years back for a price that had bought him the Plainsman. And

Duke knew it, even if he could never wholly prove it.

Gus swallowed, eased the door another fraction, listened for a moment, then slid gingerly into the reception area to the foot of the shadowed stairs.

Mason was one thing, he mused; Oliver Adams quite another. Maybe he should go take a second look over the fellow's room, check out that scented-water smell again, examine the bloodstain in closer detail. Could be there were others.

Of all the times to go offering himself as a deputy to Sheriff Malley, this was maybe not it, he thought. Still it was done now, the commitment made. He would go take that second look at Adams's room, he decided. All in the line of his new duty.

Gus was almost at the top of the stairs and into the deeper shadows of the corridor fronting the hotel rooms, when the figure slipped silently from a darkened corner of the reception area, watched the disappearing shape of the proprietor, then moved quickly to the stairs to follow.

★　★　★

'Yuh should be puttin' yuh feet up in your condition, not keepin' on them,' grunted Doc Baynam, walking slowly at the side of Sheriff Malley as they made their way along the lantern-lit board-walk. 'Appreciate yuh wantin' to keep an eye on the town, 'specially after dark, but hell, Frank, what we lookin' for exactly? Ain't a deal them bank guards missed. Turned the town over, didn't they? Whoever did the knifin' and the shootin' ain't around no more. Not unless you're settin' any store by what Gus was tellin' us.'

'Mebbe we should at that,' said Malley, pausing to try the door at Miss Peabody's millinery store. 'Maybe we should pull in every newcomer in town — that fancy Miss Dreyfus, Lawton, fella at the Plainsman — find out exactly what they're doin' here.'

'Sure,' said Doc, scanning the street ahead, 'and they might just get to tellin' yuh to mind your own business — which is what yuh should be doin' with a wound like you're carrying!'

'I'm still the law here, Doc.'

'By your fingertips, Frank. No sayin' what sorta guns Quainsley might get to summonin' out of Denver. Only hope you got now is to trust to as many standin' to yuh as possible when needed — *if* needed. Could be our killers have pulled out. Long gone. Vanished.'

Malley halted and stared at Doc. 'Gus Chappell, yourself, the judge, Quainsley's guards — t'ain't that bad a line up,' he said.

'Throw in Polly Sweet, Carbonne, Quainsley himself, even Miss Peabody here . . . goin' to look good facin' the likes of the Masons, aren't they? I don't think!'

Malley grunted and moved on slowly through the dim lights and shadows. 'It's the Masons that trouble me,' he murmured. 'Even they ain't thick-headed enough to figure for holin' up here after Narrowcot. They usually make fast for the southern borders, Mexico way. So why Jackson? Why come announcin' yourselves in the territory's biggest town?'

'Well,' pondered Doc, rubbing his chin, 'they mebbe ain't figurin' right now for bein' expected. Could be they're ridin' in, calm as yuh like, reckonin' for bein' lost in the crowd. Or it could be, o'course, they — '

'I don't wanna hear the alternatives, Doc,' interrupted Malley. 'Keep 'em to yourself. There's more than enough problems here . . . '

The sheriff's words trailed away on a weakening voice as he stared at the sprawling bulk of the Plainsman on the opposite side of the street. 'And there's one of 'em,' he croaked. 'How come there ain't a light burnin' at Gus's place this time of night?'

Doc's mouth opened, but he could only swallow.

12

'Gus ain't around,' hissed Doc at Sheriff Malley's ear once the two men had crossed the street and melted into the shadowed boardwalk fronting the Plainsman. 'Place is as quiet as the grave,' he added, squinting for some shape or hint of movement behind the hotel's darkened windows.

'Unfortunate turn of phrase, Doc!' grunted Malley, moving softly to the side of the door.

'Yeah, well, yuh can get that way in situations like this,' murmured Doc from the shadows. 'You want for me to go get some help? And don't tell me yuh can handle this. Yuh goin' to tell me just that, ain't yuh?'

'I'll handle it,' murmured Malley. 'You stay here, keep any pryin' eyes clear 'til I see what's going on in there. T'ain't like Gus to be keepin' the place in the dark at this hour.'

'That's all very well — ' began Doc.

'You move on my say-so, then yuh go get some of Quainsley's guards. No heroics. Yuh ain't bein' paid!'

Doc sighed and shrugged and eased back to the thicker shadows as Malley nodded, drew his Colt to the grip he could trust, and pushed open the door with the toe of his boot.

He winced at the exaggerated creak, waited a moment and then slipped into the musty, inky darkness.

He sniffed, catching the lingering smell of a doused lantern. Why had Gus turned out the light? *If he had.* Malley waited, the Colt steady in his hand, his gaze sharp and probing, but certain of only shapes and shadows. Anybody hidden here could stay that way for as long as he chose.

The sheriff moved on, cat-like in his steps, to the foot of the stairs, waited again and peered towards the vaguely outlined balcony corridor above him. A gap, a space, an open door to one of the rooms, but still no hint of a light, no sounds. He mounted the stairs, one careful step at a time, fearful of the creaks, his eyes working over the shadows, the Colt growing heavy in his hand.

The last step to the landing . . . the space at the open door almost beginning to beckon. Malley took a deeper breath, flexed his fingers in the grip on the gun and crept towards the room.

He had reached the threshold, halted, his boot only inches from the still wet pool of blood, his gaze already tight on the sprawled, lifeless body of Gus Chappell, when the hand reached from the darkness and settled like a manacle on the greasy, sweating flesh of his neck.

★ ★ ★

Malley groaned, writhed and twisted against the strength of the gripping hand, bounced against the door jamb and brought the Colt round in a swinging, scything swipe at his attacker.

Only then, as the man lunged away from the glinting barrel, did Malley catch the wafted smell of scented water. Adams!

Malley gasped at the searing pain and sudden throb through his wound, staggered against the jamb, slid a boot through the pool of blood and fell back from the room to the balcony railing, the flash of the steel blade in Adams's hand cutting across the darkness.

The sheriff's trigger finger worked instinctively in the mayhem, blazing a shot high into the ceiling, another into the wall at Adams's back as the man lunged on, the blade still flashing.

A third shot behind Malley's groaned agony skimmed Adams's thigh, raised a shouted curse and forced the man back.

Malley dodged, ducked against the swirl of the blade, swung himself clear of the railing, the pain pounding through his wound, blood oozing at the bandage, settled his grip on the Colt and fired another shot, this time low from the hip into Adams's bulging gut as the man thrust himself into another attack.

Adams came to a coughing, spluttering standstill, one hand across his gut, the other with the fingers locked instinctively on the handle of the knife, the arm hanging loose.

Malley stared at him defiantly, his eyes blazing with a score of questions. 'Who the hell are yuh?' he croaked, his voice grating like heeled gravel. 'What yuh doin' here?'

The Colt levelled and probed again, but now the blade was slipping from Adams's grip as he staggered a step, swayed, grinned, dribbled saliva.

'Frank!' shouted Doc from the reception area, half-a-dozen pairs of boots thudding in his wake. 'Yuh up there? What's happenin'?'

'No problem, Doc,' called Malley, stifling a wince, his gaze tightening on Adams. 'Stand back. Stay where yuh are.'

A lantern light flared into life,

throwing the shadows into a suddenly clamouring frenzy.

'Frank,' shouted Doc again, shielding his eyes against the flare, peering into the scattered darkness along the balcony. 'Yuh want some help there?'

'Not now, I don't,' returned Malley.

'Too late now, eh, Sheriff?' groaned Adams. 'Damned right . . . Too late.' His grin broadened, slid to one side, the muscles twitching, his whole body jerking through a last sway as the knife clattered to the floorboards and Adams fell back, crashing through the railings to thud to an unmoving bulk at Doc Baynam's feet.

'Ain't a deal I can do for you either, fella,' he murmured.

* * *

'So just what in the name of tarnation is goin' on in this town?' blustered Judge Maitland McArthur, pacing noisily across the Plainsman reception area, turning at the wall under a cloud of

116

cigar smoke and pacing back again. 'And will somebody quieten them nosyin' folk out there.'

One of Quainsley's bank guards nodded and disappeared into the darkened boardwalk.

'We know anythin' about the dead man?' continued the judge, examining the tip of his glowing cigar. 'What was he doin' in town? Yuh say he knifed your deputy and one of Quainsley's men, then set that scumbag yuh were holdin' free? Why? Who in hell was he, anyhow, and why did he kill Gus, f'Cris'sake? Yuh got any answers, Frank?'

'Some,' sighed Malley from his seat at the table where Doc Baynam busied himself with bandages, swabs and a bowl of hot water. 'I know why the fella we just carted out murdered Gus Chappell, but what he was doing here, hell, I ain't got a clue as yet. Not unless ... Go easy there, Doc,' he winced. 'Not unless he happened in some way to be tied in with them other new arrivals in town — Lawton and that Dreyfus woman. But, heck, that's gotta be a long shot.'

Doc Baynam grunted and moved closer to the sheriff to whisper in his ear as McArthur resumed his pacing, 'Don't for God's sake, mention the Masons.'

'Lawton's in the Palace bar,' snapped McArthur, from the other side of the room. 'Costin' the town a fortune, I shouldn't wonder. As for the woman, she's supposed to be Quainsley's guest tonight. Yuh believe that and you'll believe — '

'Quainsley's on his way now,' announced a bank guard from the doorway.

McArthur groaned and wafted a hand at the billowing cigar smoke.

'That's all we need!' croaked Doc, snipping angrily at a length of bandage. 'As if it ain't enough with this and dead bodies clutterin' the place like flies at a dung heap. I tell yuh straight up — '

'Hey, Sheriff,' called the bank guard

again from the doorway, 'fella here's just ridden in from Campsville. Says he's Lou Winters, deputy to Sheriff Ben Moore back there. Got somethin' for yuh. Real urgent. You want I should send him in?'

'Send him in,' said Malley, brushing the exasperated doc aside as he came to his feet. 'I got one awful gut-deep feelin' . . . ' he murmured, but let the words drift away on the sight of the sweat-streaked, dust-smeared deputy staggering breathlessly into the glow of the lantern light. 'Yeah,' added Malley to himself, 'and it looks as if I'm goin' to be right.'

Somewhere, deep in the desert lands to the north of Jackson, the night train's whistle pierced the silence like a siren.

13

Polly Sweet stood up, brushed the folds of her skirts into place, adjusted the expensive silk square across her shoulders, touched the falls and twirls of her hair and smiled warmly across the chilly rail-head telegraph office at Sam Swaynes, the operator.

'There she blows, Miss Polly,' he grinned, laying aside his quill, removing his eye-shade and reaching for his official railway hat. He consulted his timepiece and checked it against the office clock. 'Right on time. That's the way I like it. Get me some hours' decent sleep before the whole shebang wheels round again.' He collected his jacket from a peg and slipped it on. 'Train'll be here in a few minutes. Yuh meetin' somebody?'

'Nobody special,' said Polly, brushing at her skirts again.

'I get yuh, miss,' winked Sam over a soft grin. 'Seein' how the market's shapin' up, eh? Lookin' over the new prospects.'

'Sam Swaynes . . . ' mocked Polly. 'Shame on you to think I should be so calculatin'!'

'And calculatin's what yuh are when you've a mind, and that's a fact! Don't you go denyin' it now,' grinned Sam, priming a lantern. 'And, hell, can't say I blame yuh. Just never no tellin' who's goin' to step off the night train, is there? Every cut of every kind. I seen 'em all, and I tell yuh straight up, there's some as how I'd ship out before they got the time to spit let alone hit town. So I would.'

Sam bent to peer at the lantern wick. 'Yuh remember Skeets Carmichael? Twelve months back. Seen him the minute he stepped down, I did. Said then as how no good would come of havin' the likes of him in town. You bet I did. And we all know what happened, don't we?'

'We know,' said Polly, crossing to the office window to squint into the pitch black night. 'I sure as hell know! Still got the scars.' She ran her fingertips over a dusty pane. 'Got enough goin' on in town right now without adding to it.'

'Is that right what I hear about Gus Chappell at the Plainsman? He really dead?' Sam blinked slowly and peered again. 'Frank Malley in a shoot-out? Heard the lead flyin' up here.'

'S'right,' said Polly on a soft shiver, as she adjusted the square across her shoulders. 'Yuh ask me, there's a whole sight more goin' on in Jackson right now than's good for it. Ain't none of what's happened these past days makes any sense.'

Sam stood back from the primed lantern. 'Odd yuh should say that, Miss Polly. Had the same thoughts m'self. Get this sorta twitch in my leg here whenever there's bad weather comin' in. Ain't sayin' as how it's weather we should be frettin' on, but the twitch here says there's somethin' about, and mebbe a whole sight worse than a dead wind off the desert. I once heard tell as how — '

The night train's call and clang of its bell drowned Sam's further recollection as he collected the lantern and crossed to the door to the platform, 'Let's just hope I'm wrong, Miss, though I gotta say this old leg's gettin' to have a real nasty mind of its own . . . '

The hissing steam, clouding smoke, grind and screech of wheels on rails filled the night and scattered Sam's mutterings to the chill air. Polly settled the square at her neck and followed him to the platform where she melted silently into the deeper shadows to watch and wait.

★ ★ ★

A couple of likely-looking cattle kings there, thought Polly, following the line of passengers as they left the carriages.

Texas types, ruddy-faced, roustabout

good-timers given half a chance. She would bet to their money belts being well stacked for the pleasures of Jackson. She made a mental note to check them out at the Palace — it would certainly be the Palace for them — and let her gaze move on.

Smart-looking woman there; fashionable hat, quality cut to the dress, expensive valise; fellow accompanying her would be her husband. Keen-eyed, earnest traders definitely here on business. Of no interest, decided Polly.

Clutch of frilly, giggling girls, new recruits to the Palace chorus line; matronly mother-hen escorting them probably packed a Colt strapped to her corsets. A military type there, travelling single; customer potential. Fussy, sweating type in the check suit had to be a peddler of two-bit medicine; living on his wits and credit and all the money he could persuade folk to part with.

And that, mused Polly, hugging her arms across her in the thin night air, seemed to be that. Nothing to get excited about ... But hold it, she frowned, her arms dropping to her sides as she backed deeper into the shadows, who in the name of a bad dollar was this stepping down last from the second class? Duke Mason?

Polly stifled a shiver. Duke Mason, sure enough, large as life, and not looking a day older than when she had crossed his trail out Wisconsin way. Must be four, five years back. As long ago as that? Hell, she was getting older even if time seemed not to have brushed too close to the notorious Duke.

But since when had Mason taken to riding the iron horse? Duke had never been known to be more than a spit away from raw dust and worn leather; and just where were those scumbag brothers of his, not to mention that rattler, Charlie Drace, and his sidekick Zeb Crow? Had they split or something, wondered Polly, stifling another shiver? Well, she would step right over to him, damn it, and ask him.

No, she would not! She shrank back, her shoulders tense against the telegraph office wall. The fellow leaving the first-class carriage had his gaze tight on only one thing: Duke Mason's back. And the look in his eyes suggested this was not the moment for Polly Sweet to renew an old friendship.

And another thing, she frowned, where had she seen this sharp-suited type before? Somewhere up north? Denver way perhaps?

* * *

'Mangey story yuh carried here, Mr Winters,' said Sheriff Malley, pacing carefully across the reception area of the Plainsman to the door standing open to the night. He studied the darkness thoughtfully for a moment. 'Bad, real bad. Them Mason boys are a gut-rot. But why ain't Duke ridin' with 'em?'

'No clue here,' said Doc Baynam, tapping the pages of Ben Moore's notes. 'Just the four, accordin' to the sheriff.'

'S'right,' nodded Lou Winters. 'Just them. Real murderin' scum.'

Malley grunted and turned away from the night. 'So if them boys of Duke's are ridin' for Jackson, where's Duke? Why wasn't he with them at Campsville? Where, damn it, is he now?' He winced and put a hand to his bandaged wound. 'Anyway, my problem now, Mr Winters.' He grunted again. 'Yeah, my problem . . . So you get yourself grubbed and watered up, change of horse if you've a mind — Palace'll fix it, but keep yuh mouth shut on the news yuh brought — and then you hightail it back to Campsville, soon as yuh good and ready. And yuh can tell Ben Moore — '

Malley paused abruptly, turning again to stare into the night. 'Tell him that if them Mason rats so much as set a foot . . . ' He paused again, narrowing his gaze as Polly Sweet hurried across

127

the street. 'Now what, f'Cris'sake?' he muttered.

'Frank, thank the Lord I caught yuh,' gasped Polly, tugging desperately at the square at her shoulders as she mounted the boardwalk. 'I just come from the rail-head. Night train's in.'

'I heard it,' said Malley. 'Hey, now, you ease up there. You get to rushin' about like that, you'll do yourself an injury.'

Polly gasped again, shuddered and closed her eyes on a deep breath. 'Yeah, well, you might fast be addin' a partner to that injury yuh already got when yuh hear what I'm goin' to tell yuh.'

'I'm listenin',' croaked Malley, the colour draining from his cheeks.

Polly's eyes opened wide. 'Yuh know who's just stepped from that train back there? Duke Mason no less. And that ain't the half of it. There's somebody else . . . '

14

Matt Mason growled, spat, reeled drunkenly into the drift of boulders and flattened his back on the thickest. 'Second only to Duke that's me, and don't none of you trail rats f'get it,' he drawled, the spittle dribbling from the corner of his mouth, his hands fidgeting uselessly at his sides, fingers anxious as claws.

'Hope you ain't figurin' for drawin' on that gun of yours,' said Charlie Drace almost casually, as he concentrated on the makings of a smoke from his baccy pouch, his gaze lifting only momentarily. 'Doubt if yuh'd ever reach it, state you're in.'

Jacob Mason kicked a loose rock through the sand to the creeping shadows and spat accurately into its path. 'We're wastin' time here,' he grunted, staring at his boots. 'We rested up long enough. Time we shifted. We ride through the night we could hit Jackson soon after sun-up.' He spat again. 'Suggest we do just that, so yuh get y'self sorted, Matt, yuh hear me? No more booze. That's it. We're ridin'.'

Matt glared, dribbled but said nothing.

'Hold on there,' snapped Zeb Crow, straddling the sand at the line of the four free-standing mounts. 'I ain't so sure Jackson's still in the reckonin'.' He fixed his thumbs into his belt. 'Yuh heard what Charlie here figures — that Red James feedin' the worms right now was mebbe some part of a heist already bein' planned in the town. So where's that leave us, eh? I'll tell yuh: it leaves us snake-eyed sick on a dim outlook for what Duke's got planned. I said before, this whole fool schemin' is already blown — thanks to the soak there — and now it's double blown knowin' what we do.' Zeb stiffened. 'I say we quit. Call it off. One of us rides to Jackson, finds Duke and pulls him out before we all get killed.'

'Skinny fool talk,' drawled Matt Mason. 'Masons don't never pull out.' He belched loudly. 'T'ain't in our nature.'

'And I'll tell yuh somethin' else that ain't in your nature right now,' said Crow grimly. 'Common sense. We ride into Jackson as we are, and we're dead. I'm tellin' yuh: I can smell it.'

'Mebbe the only thing you can smell, Zeb Crow,' began Jacob, 'is yuh own — '

'Enough!' Matt Mason's voice spilled across the gathering gloom like the dregs slopped from a dropped bottle. 'I heard enough, yuh hear?' His Colt came to his hand and was levelled in an instant. 'Next man who so much as — '

'I'd go easy there if I were you,' said Drace, shafting a thin line of smoke from the corner of his mouth. 'Yuh might not have loaded that piece.'

'Yuh hankerin' for findin' out?' The Colt prodded forward.

'Let's cool it, shall we?' soothed

Jacob, taking a tentative step between Drace and his brother. 'We should mebbe think this through, weigh some odds. Hell, we got Duke down there in Jackson to think of.'

'And if he's got an ounce of sense when he hears — '

Zeb Crow's words were lost on Matt Mason's croaked growl and sudden lunge, the Colt swinging wildly through a loose shot that blazed high and wide of its intended target.

'What the hell!' groaned Jacob, his arms spreadeagling as he fell back among the boulders.

'Sonofa-goddamn-bitch . . . ' moaned Crow, his stare widening on Drace and the drawn Colt tight in his grip. 'No, don't do it, Charlie. Don't — '

But too late. Even as Matt Mason stumbled forward again, another loose shot kicking the dirt at his feet, Drace's gun roared its vicious retaliation, once, twice, spinning Mason like a top on his heels, his Colt flying uselessly from his hand, his head snapping back, mouth opening, eyes bulging.

Nobody spoke or moved as they watched Mason twitch, heard his last hiss of breath, saw the life ebb from him in the clawed fingers.

'In the name of God's hell, what yuh done there?' muttered Jacob, the sweat beading across his face. 'What yuh done, f'Cris'sake?'

'I done what's been comin' for months,' grunted Drace, holstering his Colt.

'Darn fool drew first, didn't he?' said Crow, running a hand round his neck. 'Asked for it. Would've shot yuh, Charlie, no doubtin' to that. Liquored up. Better out of it.'

'What yuh sayin'?' flared Jacob, sweat trickling to his stubble. 'That's my goddamn brother lyin' there. My brother, yuh hear? Yuh just killed one of my own, damn yuh!' He shuddered, wiped his eyes. 'Duke's brother.'

'Duke knew him for what he was,' said Drace. 'Yuh seen that for y'self.'

'Don't weigh no odds, does it, not

when it's yuh own kind?'

Crow spat and scuffed dirt. 'It's done now. No goin' back on it. We'd best bury the poor devil and then ride.'

'Ride, f'Cris'sake!' croaked Jacob. 'Where the hell we ridin'?'

'Somebody — one of us — has got to get to Jackson, find Duke, warn him. Explain all this.'

'*Explain*?' flared Jacob again. 'Yuh make it sould like we just broke a plate or somethin'. This ain't no two-bit accident. Hell, we spilled real blood here. Matt's blood. My brother's blood. Shot by one of his own partners.'

'Didn't hear no complainin' about spilled blood back there at Campsville,' sneered Drace, his stare unblinking. 'Don't hear yuh windin' yourself up over the blood of the dozen or so fellas we've gunned these past years. Blood's blood to my reckonin', and when it's bad yuh can bet yuh sweet life it's goin' to get spilled. Way of things, ain't it?'

'I wouldn't want to be standin' in your boots when yuh come to tellin' that to Duke,' croaked Jacob. 'In fact, the more I figure it, more I wouldn't want to be walkin in your tracks, let alone standin' in your boots.' He spat, wiped his face again and tightened his dark stare. 'Tell yuh somethin' for nothin', Charlie, Duke ain't goin' to take one bit kindly — '

'Duke and me'll take our chances like we always have,' said Drace. 'I ain't for sayin' no more on the matter. Now, we goin' to clear up here and then ride?'

'The three of us? To Jackson?' frowned Crow.

'Where else? Duke'll be waitin' for us, won't he?'

The sweat on Jacob's face turned suddenly icy.

Zeb Crow was aware for the first time that night that the darkness had closed in.

★　★　★

Duke Mason finished his measure of whiskey in one swift gulp, replaced the

135

glass on the table and roved his gaze anxiously over the crowded bar of the Palace hotel.

He had been lucky to get the corner table and keep it to himself. Ideally placed, he thought, with its clear view across the room to the main doors. But only ideal for now. A few more minutes and he would have to move, go find himself a cheap, back alley bed for the night; somewhere he could think, rest up, be alone and unnoticed. Somewhere a whole sight less public and glittery than the Palace, and somewhere, damn it, where he could get to reshaping his plans.

Just what in hell was happening in Jackson, anyhow, he pondered, his fingers idling at the empty glass? The Plainsman deserted, locked and under guard; Gus Chappell dead, murdered; the sheriff in a shoot-out; talk through the town of dead bodies, maybe some deeper threat still lurking — this was no time to be planning a raid on the territory's richest bank.

So was he for waiting on the boys and then pulling out some place south, holing-up a while till things in Jackson looked and felt a deal quieter, or would he sit it out, bide his time, watch events and strike when the advantage slid his way?

Might be something to be said for a helping of civic confusion. Could be the law would be so preoccupied with other matters that Duke Mason and company would hardly warrant a second glance, until it was too late and they were gone, the better part of the bank's money with them.

The fingers tensed and stiffened, Mason's eyes narrowed and stared hard at the man who had just walked into the bar from the boardwalk.

Chad Lawton of all people!

Mason lowered his head a fraction, at the same time shifting the angle of his gaze as he watched Lawton hesitate for a moment, look round the customers as if expecting to pinpoint an expected face, then make his way through the babble of drinkers to the bar.

What the hell was Lawton doing in Jackson? Not looking well for one thing; there was a pale, pinched look across his features, the grey pallor of a worried man, far removed from the Chad Lawton he had known, crossed and hated in Denver.

But Lawton's gaze had not ventured to the corner table. Lucky — but not a luck to be pushed, thought Mason, coming carefully to his feet and making a slow, inconspicuous way to the door.

He would hit the street and disappear for the night; go bury himself till first light. And by then, if they were holding to time, the boys would be here and they could sneak away south together. Sneak it would have to be, he reckoned. Wherever Lawton walked, big guns, mean guns, were never far behind. He had no wish to tangle, especially not in Jackson at this time.

The Mason gang raid on the Western Central and South Peaks bank was off — for now. The boys would simply have to abide by the rules as he laid them down. No arguing, no dissent.

Duke Mason seemed unaware of the two men, who slipped quietly from the shadowed frontage of Bright's mercantile to follow at a safe distance as he headed for the dimly lit back alleys in search of a bed.

15

'I got him watched. He won't go far, leastways not tonight. Tomorrow might be different.' Sheriff Malley winced at a stab of pain deep in his shoulder wound, paused a moment, then continued carefully across the floor of his office to the dark, dusty window. 'Ain't a deal more I can do 'til sun-up.'

'And then?' asked Louis Quainsley brusquely.

'Then,' said Malley, turning from the window to face the banker and Doc Baynam seated either side of the cluttered desk, 'I'll look at the situation again.'

'In other words, wait and see,' snapped Quainsley. 'Do nothin' 'til somebody makes a move.'

Malley stiffened. 'Yuh got a better way?'

Quainsley drummed the fingers of a

hand impatiently on the desk. 'Perhaps not, but having the Mason gang hovering on my porch ain't exactly a comfortable outlook. They have a reputation, all of them, and not very savoury at that. It ain't good for business or the town to have gunslingers prowlin'.'

'We got only Duke at the moment,' said Doc quietly.

'Just so,' agreed Quainsley. 'But you don't suppose, surely, that he's here alone for a rest from the others. That's hardly likely. The Masons, from what I hear of them always operate as a gang. They're close, tight as flies on dung, and Duke Mason keeps it that way. The others will be here soon, you can bet on it.' He eyed Malley closely. 'You could make sure Mason leaves town at first light — the very first light. At gunpoint perhaps?'

'Sure, I could,' shrugged Malley. 'And have him and his sidekicks back in town faster than I can say it — only this time they wouldn't be here for the scenery or the company: they'd be here to kill, maim, rape, loot, whatever came easiest to hand. I ain't takin' that kinda risk, Mr Quainsley. Not no how I ain't, not even for you.'

Quainsley grunted, flattened his hand on the table and came to his feet. 'I could, of course, get my own boys to do the job. They'd welcome it. The sort of thing they like getting their teeth into.'

'You could do that, sure,' said Malley, stifling a wince. 'I ain't exactly in a fit state to do much about stoppin' yuh, savin' to remind I *am* the law; I wear the badge. Yuh heard what's happened here in town tonight. Gus Chappell dead; we got his killer, but the hotel's closed and, if yuh want my opinion, we ain't heard the last of whoever that fella Adams truly was. Could be he was here in advance of . . . ' Malley spread his arms. 'Who knows? Mebbe he was tied in with Chad Lawton.'

'So you're sayin' we stay clear of Mason,' said Quainsley. 'Let him be 'til we see his intent. That it?'

'Precisely it,' nodded Malley.

'I hope you know what you're doing.' Doc Baynam cleared his throat, leaned back in the chair and folded his arms. 'What can you tell us that's decent about the woman yuh entertained to dinner tonight?'

'I trust you're not suggestin' — ' blustered Quainsley.

'I ain't suggestin' nothin'. I can imagine. I'm askin'.' Doc's gaze sharpened. 'That fiancé of hers arrive on the night train?'

'I believe so,' said Quainsley, coming to his full height. 'Miss Dreyfus said he was due. Staying at the Palace. Naturally.'

Doc unfolded his arms and leaned forward. 'She give yuh a name?' he asked sharply.

Quainsley shrugged loosely. 'Carter, I think. I took no particular note. Not really interested. Why should I be?'

''Cus Polly Sweet saw a man she believes to be Miras Carter leave the train tonight,' said Malley, turning back

143

to the window. 'If it is Carter, she's crossed him before. She don't recall exactly where, but — '

'I don't see that some vague recollection by Polly Sweet is any good reason for adding to the problem we already got with the prospect of the Masons hitting town,' said Quainsley impatiently.

Doc slapped a hand on the desk. 'Sorta company Polly's sometimes been obliged to keep is always worth notin', seein' as how most of it slid straight out of a rattlers' nest!'

Quainsley took a deep breath. 'I think that is going to be another matter for the law to be looking to. Meantime, I'll have my men keep an eye on Mr Carter — *and* stay watchful for the Masons. They are the problem, Sheriff, make no mistake.' He adjusted his frockcoat and reached for his hat. 'Sun-up is going to be critical, I fancy. That your opinion, gentlemen?'

★ ★ ★

Duke Mason smiled softly to himself from the depths of the hugging shadows. Give it another minute, he thought, and he would put a flame to a cheroot, let the shape of him be seen, his exact whereabouts duly noted by the two men who were doing their best to follow him.

Hell, they deserved a break!

He smiled again and relaxed, his gaze sharp as a hunting hawk's as he watched the two men hover uncertainly on the boardwalk across the street. Sheriff's men, he reckoned, deputies, and new to the job by the look of the way they were going about shadowing him.

But that, he pondered, the smile fading as he eased into the still deeper darkness, was hardly the point. The point was, he had been recognized; somebody here in Jackson had spotted him in the time it had taken for him to cross from the rail-head to the Palace bar and reported his, or maybe her, suspicions to the sheriff.

Bad news piling on bad news. If he had needed any confirmation of his presence in Jackson not being the smartest of ideas right now, he surely had it.

The law was sitting on his butt.

Somewhere back there in his office, one already hard-pushed, tired-eyed sheriff — wounded into the bargain, he had heard — was figuring on why Duke Mason was in town, but convinced without needing to think it that he would not be alone for much longer and that the rest of the gang had been raising trail dirt for some time.

Hence the two mule-heads shadowing him. The sheriff was taking no chances between now and sun-up.

Mason reached into his pocket for the cheroot, scratched a match into life and let the flame flare for a moment before killing it behind a cloud of smoke. He waited, watching the men on the boardwalk turn quickly at the flaring light, the curling smoke, exchange words, part and head across the street, one to the left, one to the right.

Predictable, just as he would have expected.

He waited another fifteen seconds, counting them down below his breath, before blowing more smoke, heeling the cheroot where he stood and stepping sharply into the narrow alley facing him and back to the street.

He glanced round, noting the lights at windows, catching the few sounds, the occasional resident hurrying home, the bar girl out there taking the air, smoking a cigar.

Rear of the Palace, he decided. There would almost certainly be outbuildings there, some place to hole-up through the darkest hours till the first hint of light, then he would head for the far end of town where the trail from the north joined with the main street. Be there when the boys rode in.

He smiled again, crossed the street and disappeared.

★　★　★

There were outbuildings at the rear of the Palace, two secured against prying eyes and anxious fingers, a third, smaller and no longer in day-to-day use with a broken window and a loose hanging door.

Duke Mason had it spotted in seconds.

He was at the door and easing it carefully aside on its single rusted hinge when he heard the softest fall of a step to his right and saw a shadow move.

One of the sheriff's men, he wondered, a hand already settling on the butt of his Colt? Unlikely. They would still be fathoming the smoke-filled shadows and heeled cheroot. So how many deputies did the sheriff have at his call? No matter, this one had a deal more about him. He was gentle on his feet, patient, watchful.

In fact, a whole sight too watchful for Duke Mason's comfort.

16

Another step, soft and easy; the shadow shifted again, this time reaching like a giant hand to where Mason waited, as still and silent as a stone, by the broken outbuilding door.

How close did the fellow figure on getting, he wondered? Had he seen Mason, or was he just being cautious? Was he alone, or did he have a partner working along of him? And why was he here; had he watched Mason cross the street?

Mason's fingers tightened on the butt of his gun as he drew it slowly, smoothly, from its holster. No outright shooting if possible, he decided. Too much noise. Single shot would be enough to bring half the town scurrying to the Palace.

The shadow had halted, but Mason could feel the eyes watching him, concentrated for the one careless movement that would —

Mason tensed, felt the first trickle of a cold sweat down his spine as he became chillingly aware of a movement, another presence, behind him.

'I figure this for bein' about as far as you're goin', mister,' said the unseen man to the back of Mason's head. 'So why don't yuh just lay down the piece and come nice and quiet to that cosy cell waitin' on yuh back there at Sheriff Malley's office?'

Mason did not move. He flexed his fingers over the gun butt, steadied his balance. 'You happen to be the law here-abouts, mister?' he asked casually. 'That your sidekick I fancy watchin' there?'

'Yeah, we're the law — Jackson town private law, bank law, courtesy Western Central and South Peaks.'

'Bank guards,' muttered Mason.

'Who's botherin'? You're roped, mister, and if you're carryin' the name Duke Mason, a rope is surely where you're goin' to end. Now, let's move — '

The last sound of the man's voice was splintered and drowned in the roar of Mason's Colt as he blazed two fast shots directly into the bulk behind the shadow, then, swinging round blazed again, this time aware, only for seconds, of the open-mouthed look of shock on the guard's face as lead burned into him and threw him back among the clutter of the outbuildings.

Mason spat, wiped the sweat from his face and was moving even as the first of the babble of shouting erupted in the Palace bar. He shrank back to the shadows, waited, spat again.

Which way, damn it?

The street would be teeming in minutes; no chance of crossing it. The same went for the back alleys. The main street buildings, sheds, shacks and outbuildings would be searched thoroughly . . .

The shouting grew louder. Doors opened, banged shut. Feet pounded along boardwalks.

'Sheriff's on his way!' echoed a shouted call.

'Shots came from back of the Palace.'

'Easy as yuh go. Talk is Duke Mason's in town.'

'Somebody go get my buffalo gun. I'll blast the sonofabitch clean outa the territory!'

The voices jostled like a clutch of roosting crows. Lights began to blaze as the town stirred from its broken sleep; lanterns swung; somebody lit a torch and held the flare high to the night to send the shadows leaping and sprawling along the street.

Mason had seen and heard enough. His situation was getting trickier by the second. Another few minutes and he might find himself outflanked.

'Back of the Palace, lads. That's where we need to be.'

The shout went up to another surge of mumbled oaths and curses.

'We'll settle this right where we find the rat!'

Now it really was time to move thought Mason, listening to the crowd begin to gather, seeing the lights swing and dance. He probably had less than two minutes to make good his escape. Miss out and he had the prospect of an already fevered lynch mob baying at his heels.

He settled his grip on the Colt, wiped the sweat from his face and slid away from the shadows to the hotel's rear door. Only one thing for it, he had reckoned, he would have to go bury himself in the last place the mob would figure for him hiding — in one of the Palace's luxurious rooms!

He reached the door, heaved on a gentle sigh and grunt as it opened to his touch and slipped into a dark empty corridor. The door closed and bolted firmly behind him, he waited, one ear on the gathering noise outside among the outbuildings, the other on the sounds beyond the corridor.

'Damnit, we got two dead men here,' somebody shouted from the disused shack.

'Ain't no sign of Mason.'

'Keep lookin'. He can't have gotten far.'

Mason moved on, almost on tiptoe now. Another door to his left, one to the right, both storerooms, he reckoned. The door ahead of him had to lead to one of the hotel's public areas. But which? Hell, supposing he walked clear into the bar!

He waited again, listening for the slightest sounds: a soft buzz of voices, clink of glasses, bottles, but no sounds of the girls, nothing of the piano. Most folk were concentrated on the activity in the street, he reckoned, a slow grin edging at his lips at the thought of the confusion and frustration.

The grin faded just as quickly. No time now to get to counting his luck, not yet, not in Jackson, a place he was fast coming to wish he had never thought of, much less set eyes on. This was the town that was supposed to be swinging the wings to his future. Sure, but it might yet be lifting the lid on his coffin.

He assured himself of his grip on the Colt and turned the doorknob carefully.

★ ★ ★

He was into a shadowed area somewhere beneath the spread of the main staircase to the first-floor rooms. Pails, besoms, boxes of cleaning cloths, mops, spare glasses, a broken chair, a three-legged table cluttered his way as he stepped gingerly towards a narrow flight of back stairs.

He blinked, paused a moment to catch the murmur of voices in the main bar, the still pounding footfalls across the boardwalks, shouts from the outbuildings as the search went on, then moved slowly to the stairs, testing each step against the creak of boards.

How many rooms were occupied, he wondered, how many doors unlocked? He would have little time to select a room; it would come down to the first door that opened.

Another pause as he reached the top of the stairs and stared down the long corridor above the bar and reception area. A dozen doors, all closed on what seemed to be silent rooms. He would select the nearest; this one no more than an arm's length away.

Locked, damn it!

Try the next. Locked.

The third door. Locked.

He began to sweat, felt the breath tighten in his chest, the Colt growing heavier in his hand.

He paused again, his fingers reluctant to take a grip on the knob of the fourth door.

Footsteps now. Two men heading up the main stairs. Hell!

The fourth door was locked.

Sweat dripped from Mason's chin as he lunged at the fifth door, teeth clenched, eyes round and staring, turned the knob and almost lost his grip as the door opened slowly, smoothly with no more than a whispered creak.

He slid like a snake into the darkened room and leaned back on the door, his eyes closed, the Colt hanging low and loose at his side.

Made it, damn it! The luck had held. Now all he had to do was sit tight, let the few hours till first light pass quietly and keep a careful watch for the boys riding in. Once they reached town . . .

'Miras, that you there?'

The woman's voice cut across the darkness like the touch of steel.

17

'He ain't left town, and he won't, not 'til he's got his brothers here and the rest of the gang round him. That much is for certain.'

Doc Baynam crossed the sheriff's office to the open door to the boardwalk and the dimly lit, deep-shadowed street. 'Duke Mason's loyal to his own kind if nothin' else.'

'Hah!' bellowed Maitland McArthur. 'Well, we'll see about his so-called loyalty when he's walking to the gallows — his pathetic gang along of him. 'You can take that for certain!'

Sheriff Malley sighed, leaned back in his chair and closed his eyes.

'What yuh reckon, Quainsley?' added the judge, addressing the bank president. 'A hangin' suit you and your men? I'll sure as hell see as Mason gets it.'

Louis Quainsley turned a pale, drawn but anger-tight face to McArthur, glared at him for a moment, then let the gaze move on to the sheriff and Doc Baynam. 'Where is the sonofabitch now?' His eyes darkened. '*Where is Duke Mason?* Answer me that, will you, any one of you?'

'It's like I said — ' began the doc.

'I heard what you said, Doc,' glowered Quainsley, 'and mebbe you're right. Probably are. But that ain't enough. Not by a half it ain't. I want Mason *now*, before this night is through. And I am not interested in a hanging. That is too good, too damned easy.'

'Well, you hold up there,' began Doc again, crossing back to the desk and into the spread of soft lantern light. 'You ain't alone in wantin' Mason brought to book, and fast. We all do, not least the kin of the two men who died out there tonight. They got all the good reasons you're ever likely to need for wantin' Mason, but we ain't goin' to

159

do it by pullin' this town apart plank by plank. We start down that road and there'll be hell let loose and before yuh can say supper's up, we'll have a lynchin' or mebbe worse.'

Doc paused a moment, his grey eyes moist and glistening. 'I know, I seen men lather themselves up like that before. You let a devil loose and you'll have a street out there lookin' like a blood tub.'

'I lost two good men tonight,' continued Quainsley, his stare suddenly wild. 'I've already lost Hank Scots, and we've seen Gus Chappell murdered outright. Then there's that fella Adams . . . Now there's Mason, this Carter you're frettin' over . . . There's the Mason gang still to come . . . What's with this town f'Cris'sake? Where are we goin'? What's happenin'?'

'I'll tell yuh what's happenin',' said McArthur, shifting his bulk uncomfortably. 'We're sittin' around here when we should be doin'. Talkin's got its time and place, but this ain't it. I'm for the law — you know that well enough — but we got a disease festerin' here, and I think you're right, Quainsley: where are we goin', just what is happenin'? We want answers, and we ain't goin' to get within a spit of them sittin' here like — '

'We will do this my way, or yuh get yourselves another man behind this badge,' said Malley, his eyes opening like the slow drawing back of tired blinds. 'Struttin' and shoutin' about ain't goin' to get nobody no place. We need sun-up. We need to see all this in the light of day — and I mean see, with both eyes and a clear head.'

'Meantime,' sneered Quainsley, 'I suppose we're all goin' to sit around, keep talkin', stay waitin' until there's nothin' we ain't — '

'Somebody here ain't sittin' about,' said Doc from the open door. He took a step to the boardwalk. 'Carbonne from the Palace, scurryin' this way like he's got a rattler sewn in his pants!'

'I'm tellin' yuh he's there — right there in the woman's room. Holdin' Miss Dreyfus hostage. Says he'll shoot her first fella tries to take him. And believe you me, he ain't kiddin'.'

Bertram Carbonne glanced hysterically over the faces watching him before swamping his sweat-soaked cheeks and jowls in a vast polka-dot bandanna.

'It's an outrage,' growled Maitland McArthur.

'What did I tell you?' said Quainsley, tightening his hands behind his back as he swayed to and fro on his heels. 'What have I said all along? You give a man like Mason a rein's length of leather and he'll take a mile. Proves it, don't it? Proves the whole point of what I've been saying. And you, Sheriff Malley, should have been listening. Now what are we goin' to do? Will somebody tell me?'

'Cut out the gloatin' and sneerin' for a start!' snapped Doc Baynam. He turned to Malley. 'What yuh reckon, Frank?'

'Run through it again, will yuh, Bertram? The details this time. Ain't fussed over the emotion.'

Carbonne shuddered, ran the bandanna over his face and neck again, wiped the palms of his hands and swallowed noisily. 'Do I have to?' he croaked.

'Get to it!' cracked the Doc. 'Sheriff's waitin'. We're *all* waitin', damnit!'

Carbonne nodded. 'Soon as folk heard the shootin' back of the hotel, they started clearin' the bars, reception and that. Kinda half scared, half curious, I suppose. Anyhow, when we got out back, there was nothin' save the bodies. Your men, Quainsley. Then, o'course, the search got underway, and I figured that for bein' that so far as I was concerned.'

Carbonne began to ooze sweat. 'I was in the hotel bar when a newly arrived resident, Mr Miras Carter, came to me with the alarmin' news that he had tried

163

to enter Miss Dreyfus's room — well, naturally enough, he is the woman's fiancé, after all — only to find the door locked and a man, Mason, announcin' from *inside* the room that he is holdin' Miss Dreyfus hostage against his own life and safe passage from town when he's good and ready, and that he wants to see the sheriff immediately.'

Carbonne swallowed again, twisting the bandanna through his fingers. 'So I came straight over,' he concluded. 'And I suggest we don't waste no more time. Anythin' might happen to that woman. Anythin' . . . And it ain't good for business, not at a place like the Palace it ain't.'

Doc Baynam adjusted his hat angrily. Quainsley tugged at the lapels of his frockcoat. Maitland McArthur lit a large cigar and blew a cloud of smoke before groaning, 'Hell's been let loose!'

Malley came to his feet wearily, one hand settling on his bandaged shoulder wound. 'Where's Carter now?' he asked.

'In the bar,' said Carbonne, from behind the fluttering folds of the bandanna. 'Seems to have teamed up with another new resident, Mr Lawton.'

'You bet he has,' murmured Malley, crossing to the office window. 'Right,' he said, his voice lifting, 'here's what yuh do. I want the Palace cleared. Everybody out. Residents, staff, girls. Everybody.'

'But I can't just — ' protested Carbonne.

Malley's face darkened. 'Do it! Take the keys to the Plainsman, open it up and move your guests and operations there 'til further notice. Judge McArthur here will help yuh get organized.'

'Well, I don't know . . . ' The judge huffed for a moment under Malley's withering gaze.

The sheriff turned to Quainsley. 'Round up the men you've got left and send them to me. They're under my orders from here on. Then get back to that bank of yours and don't leave it. Understood?'

Quainsley shrugged. 'If you think it will do any good . . . '

'I do,' snapped Malley, 'so just get to it, eh?' He turned to Doc Baynam. 'Doc, you stay along of me. We got a busy night ahead — what's left of it.'

'And the Mason gang?' asked Quainsley. 'What about them?'

Malley glanced at the clock on the wall. 'If they're ridin' hard, they'll be here in four hours. We'll be ready.'

'You'd better be right,' said McArthur darkly.

'I better had,' grunted Malley.

★　★　★

Chad Lawton licked his lips and watched himself going through the nervous action in the mirror facing him at the back of the sprawling Palace bar. He was conscious of Miras Carter following his every twitch and gesture in the reflection.

'Can't just leave her, can we?' murmured Lawton, still watching the reflection. 'Not now we've come this far. Hell, no, we couldn't do that. Yuh wouldn't, would you?'

Carter examined the measure of whiskey on the bar in front of him. 'Can't get to her, can we? Leastways, not without spitting lead with Duke Mason, and I ain't for that. We get ourselves into that sorta showdown and we lose everythin' — mebbe our lives. We keep clear of Mason and leave him to the sheriff and half the town, and we might, just might — '

'What, just the two of us? Hell, no. We already lost Adams, and Red ain't shown since he was sprung, so that don't leave a deal, does it? Not by my reckonin' it don't.'

Carter tapped a thoughtful finger on the bar. 'It leaves us, my friend, if we act fast enough, against a bank nobody's watchin' or even interested in. A bank, you might say, with its doors wide open to those who happen to be waitin'. Yuh reckon?'

'There's still the guards, though,' said Lawton. 'They ain't for messin' with. I been watchin' them.' He twitched his shoulders anxiously. 'Fact is, it's all fallin' apart, ain't it? How come Adams managed to get himself into a fight with that Sheriff Malley? I warned him to keep it cool. What he wanted to go tanglin' with that Plainsman hotel owner for I'll never know. Hell! And what's happened to Red James, f'Cris'sake? He was supposed to be here hours ago. And now there's Mason. It can only be a matter of time before the rest of his gang arrives. And then . . .'

'Could be Mason's done us a real favour.'

'How come?'

'Well, now,' mused Carter, bringing the finger into action again, 'if I were the sheriff here, what would I do in this situation? Empty the Palace for a start. But with folk confused and the town smarting under Mason's hold on it . . . what better diversion for the likes of

168

us? Sheriff's goin' to want every able-bodied man standin' by him against the arrival of Mason's sidekicks.'

'Sure,' insisted Lawton, 'but why did Mason ride in on the night train alone? Answer me that.'

Carter rested the finger. 'Any one of a dozen reasons, I guess. But, for me, knowin' the way Duke Mason figures things, I'd say he's here to rob the Western Central and South Peaks bank. Wouldn't you?'

'But — '

'Your attention, please, ladies and gentlemen,' announced Carbonne from the entrance to the bar. 'Thank you, thank you.' He smiled nervously. 'Due to circumstances beyond our control, and in the interests of safety, it has been decided by Sheriff Malley and Judge McArthur that the hotel be cleared of its residents and customers. I'd be grateful therefore . . . '

'Well, ain't that just a timely coincidence?' murmured Carter behind a slow, satisfied grin.

18

Geraldine Dreyfus adjusted her dress across her exposed shoulder, glanced quickly at the man watching her, then turned her back on him and stared out of the window into the empty, silent street. 'You can look all you like, Mr Mason, I can't stop you, but that is all you'll get. Bear it in mind.' Her voice was cold, the words as chipped as ice.

'Yes, ma'am, yuh got it,' grinned Mason cynically. 'Would I, a decent, upstandin', God-fearin' man, think any other?'

'You would, probably are, and there's nothing decent let alone God-fearing about Duke Mason.'

Mason eased himself on to the bed and leaned back against the piled pillows. 'You got that for a fact, ma'am? Or are yuh just sittin' alongside the rumours?'

The woman turned slowly, her gaze as honed as a skinning blade. 'I know of you well enough,' she said quietly. 'Your reputation rides ahead of you, as does your notoriety and the price on your head for Heaven knows how many killings. I have no wish to keep such company.'

'All things bein' equal, o'course, yuh ain't got no choice right now, have yuh, Miss hoity-toity Dreyfus? Or may I call you Geraldine?' Mason tittered and laid his Colt at his side, smoothing the folds of the sheet clear of its hammer. 'I wouldn't pursue that line of talk if I were you,' he said flatly, his gaze deepening. 'I might get to wantin' to prove it, and that would be a shame. Yuh follow my meanin'?'

Geraldine Dreyfus stiffened, but remained silent, her stare chillingly unblinking.

'Meantime,' began Mason again, 'it's time — '

'Time you came to your senses, Mr Mason, and faced a few realities. One:

this hotel has now been vacated, we are here alone, but surrounded, you may be sure. I doubt if you will walk out of the place alive. Two, I have friends here in Jackson — '

'Ah, yes,' smiled Mason, 'I was goin' to ask about Miras Carter. And was that Chad Lawton I heard along of him at your door? You bet, eh? Now what would a classy filly like y'self be doin' mixin' with them scumbags? Don't tell me it's love?'

The woman drew her lips to a tight line as she stifled a reaction, waited a moment, staring directly into Mason's eyes, then said quietly, carefully, 'I wouldn't tangle there if I were you.'

Mason tittered again to himself. 'Well, yuh sure as hell ain't me, that's for rock-bottom certain, but as for tanglin', I'm goin' to take a wild guess here. You just hear me out, lady, while we still got the time.'

The woman stayed silent, still staring, the merest shimmer of a beading of sweat across her brow.

'I figure it this way,' continued Mason, stretching his legs the length of the bed, 'Miras Carter and Chad Lawton in Jackson t'gether, livin' real smooth at the Palace Hotel. Now that raises suspicions. Two rats in one box ain't there for their health — so what's the attraction? Pretty as yuh are, ma'am, t'ain't all your shapely self they're lookin' to lay their hands on. Right?'

'You are disgusting!'

'Yeah, well, mebbe . . . The main attraction for a pair the likes of Carter and Lawton is same as its always been: money. Big money; all the money a man can handle. Now, where would you reckon for that kinda pile bein' held in a place like Jackson? Don't need any guesses, do you? 'Course not. So what's your part in the proposed heist, Miss Dreyfus? Where do you figure, or have yuh already done your job? I'll be listenin'; take yuh time.

'Oh, and just so's I get to feelin' a whole lot more comfortable, be grateful if you'd slip that derringer from yuh garter. I can see the bulge from here, and it spoils the view.'

* * *

'Yuh hear that, Frank?' called Doc Baynam across the suddenly crowded, smoke-filled sheriff's office. 'Just had news from out at the Pemberton spread back of White Rocks: three riders passed through there at sundown. Ridin' hard. Headin' clear for Jackson. Yuh reckon them for the Mason gang?'

'Only three?' answered Malley, from the gun cabinet at the far end of the room.

'Three have been sighted, three's what we got,' shrugged Doc. 'Yuh want for me to ride out, go take a look for m'self?'

'No, you stay here, Doc. Round up Mac Downie. Send him. He knows the country. And tell him not to hang about. One sighting, time and place. That's all we need.'

174

'Yuh got it,' called Doc, heading for the boardwalk.

'Right,' said the sheriff, turning to the group of men at his back, handing out Winchesters as he addressed them, 'now here's the way of it if you fellas are still of a mind.'

'We're with yuh, Frank,' said one man.

'All the way, whatever it takes,' added another.

'Ain't no two-bit gunslingers gettin' to carve up our town,' grunted a third. 'Over my dead body!'

'Let's make sure it don't come to that,' said Malley, piling boxes of cartridges on his desk. 'Help yourselves.' He waited, watching the men carefully. 'All right, once you're leaded up to your satisfaction, yuh work in pairs — always in pairs, understand, no goin' out on a limb 'til yuh forced.

'Two of yuh take up positions back of the Palace. Nobody in, nobody out. Two of yuh work the back alleys. Four of yuh similarly the main street; two one side, two the other. Try not to lose contact, but don't break the pattern savin' on my own or Doc Baynam's orders. And keep a close eye on the folk we've transferred to the Plainsman. Don't let 'em stray. You'll cross Quainsley's men from time to time. They're under my orders.'

Malley fell silent, watchful, glancing quickly over the faces of the men. 'You're all deputies now, representin' the law and Jackson. Don't let either of them down. Any questions?'

'How long we got, Frank? When are we expectin' the scum?'

'Yuh heard what Doc said, they passed White Rocks at sundown. So . . . ' He glanced at the clock. 'If they keep up the pace, we'll see 'em in roughly two hours. I'm pretty sure they'll ride in at first light. Stay awake!'

'What yuh goin' to do about Duke and the woman he's holdin'?'

'Leave Duke Mason to me: he ain't goin' no place.' Malley laid a hand on his throbbing shoulder. 'Time to get to it. And remember, no big deal heroics. I ain't lookin' for boostin' the Boot Hill business, 'ceptin' in selected cases! Yuh get my meanin', I hope. On your way. And thanks, and good luck.'

The men shouldered their weapons and moved away in the still dark night. Malley watched them go from the shadowed boardwalk, wondering how many he would next see still standing, how many bleeding, how many dead.

'Don't dwell on it, Frank,' said Doc, stepping silently to the sheriff's side. 'It's their town as much as yours. They know the risks.' He tamped the bowl of his pipe. 'Mac Downie's on his way. He's clear what to do.' He sighed softly. 'And now?' he asked.

'Now we get to disturbin' Mr Mason's beauty sleep! Grab yourself a Winchester.'

★ ★ ★

Duke Mason smiled softly to himself as he crossed the hotel room once again to stand at the side of the window, glance quickly into the empty street below, then at Geraldine Dreyfus seated on the stool at the dressing-table, her gaze seemingly lost and vacant on the images reflected in the mirror. Or was it, he wondered? Maybe she was simply thinking, regretting, feeling sorry for herself.

Or plotting.

His smile faded. She was plotting, deep as a skulking lioness, you could bet on it, he thought. Figuring just how she was going to get back to her partnership with Miras Carter and Chad Lawton. The stakes were too high to pass over. And, in any case, he reckoned, this lady was not for losing out on this or any other investment. It was not in her razor-sharp nature.

'Doin' some heavy thinkin' there, ma'am,' he said lazily. 'That bad, is it? Don't tell me I'm suddenly the bad apple that's spoiled the whole barrel.'

'I could think of infinitely more appropriate and filthier comparisons!'

clipped the woman, her gaze still on the mirror.

'Bet yuh could at that,' grinned Mason, watching the street again. ''Course, there is a way out of your predicament.' He paused, conscious of the flick of a sidelong glance. 'Yuh could join forces with me and my boys. You'd be real welcome.'

'Hah! I'd sooner bed down with a rattler!'

'That might be nice goin' for the rattler, ma'am, but a whole sight mule-headed on your part. Figure it: if I'm right, and I reckon I am, that Carter and Lawton have got their eyes on the bank, question you're tryin' to answer is: what are they goin' to do about me now that I'm in the mess I am? Right? I'm right.

'Well, yuh want my opinion in one spit, they'll either go ahead and grab what they can from the bank, or back off and ride out.' Mason paused again before adding, 'Either way, lady, they ain't goin' to hang about Jackson waitin' on you.'

Geraldine Dreyfus stared deep into the mirror, her eyes wide, round, Summer-sky blue and unblinking, her lips tight in a defiantly silent line.

'On the other hand,' continued Mason, 'me and my boys are — '

'And what precisely are you doing in Jackson, Mr Mason?' snapped the woman. 'Why are you holed-up here like a rat in a trap, and just where are these famous boys?' She tossed the curls of her long chestnut hair and scoffed cynically. 'I would simply love to hear more of your ridiculous fantasizing!'

Mason resisted the temptation to seize a handful of the woman's hair, knot it in his grip and force her head back till she gasped. 'Well, now,' he began quietly, licking at a surge of sweat, 'and so yuh shall, lady, so yuh shall — hear how me and the boys are plannin' to do exactly what you and your two-bit sidekicks have in mind: rob the bank. Difference bein', o'course, we ain't goin' to fail. Nossir.

The Mason gang don't ever fail . . . '

'Mason!' came the clipped, cold shout from the street. 'Shift yuh butt and show yuh face. Get to the window there, open it and listen to what I gotta say. No messin'. Otherwise, we'll blow yuh to hell. Do it, damn yuh. Now!'

19

'Goin' to say this once and once only,' called Sheriff Malley from the street, watching through keen, narrowed eyes as the window at the softly lit hotel room slid open to Mason's touch.

'Then you'd best get to it, and fast,' shouted the gunslinger before slipping out of sight.

'Sonofan-arrogant-bitch!' murmured Doc at Malley's side. 'What the hell does he think he's doin'?'

Malley grunted and took a deep breath. 'We know yuh got Miss Dreyfus there,' he called again. 'I want some assurance she's safe.'

'Alive and kickin' — see for yourself,' said Mason, pushing the woman into full view at the open window. 'Satisfied?'

'You all right, ma'am?' queried Doc.

'She's fine,' snapped Mason, dragging the woman back to the shadows.

'Now, get on with it, will yuh?'

Doc cursed quietly to himself.

'I ain't a notion of where yuh think all this is headin',' began Malley, 'but yuh should know we ain't for dealin' none. Best I can offer yuh right now is a guarantee yuh won't get shot between the hotel and the jail providin' yuh throw down yuh gun and step out now, real quiet, Miss Dreyfus along of yuh. That's a promise.

'After that . . . Well, I hear you and your boys are wanted for robbery in Narrowcot, and yuh should know yuh brothers and them other sidekicks got themselves in a whole heap of trouble back at Campsville. I hear three men died under yuh brother Matt's gun, one bein' the sheriff's deputy. That's serious, Duke, real serious. So you can be assured that the minute Matt rides in here — as I'm sure he will — he and his partners will be taken in and penned tight as ticks. That, too, is a promise. I make myself clear?'

There was a long full minute of chilling silence, when the space at the window stayed empty, the street eerily deserted, save for the waiting shapes of Sheriff Malley and Doc Baynam, their shadows reaching ahead of them like flat black pillars.

'What's with the rat?' whispered Doc anxiously. 'He surely ain't thinkin' of makin' a fight of it, is he?'

'Just that!' clipped Malley as two fast shots from the window kicked the dirt not a yard from where he stood. 'Take cover! Back to the boardwalk.'

'That's my answer to your worthless promises,' yelled Mason. 'Like yourself, I ain't for dealin' none, but since you're statin' positions, here's mine: one, yuh stay clear of this hotel. No attemptin' to enter it. First hint I get of unwelcome visitors, the woman here suffers. And I mean, suffers.

'Two, minute my brothers and partners hit town, yuh bring 'em here to me. No messin'. Yuh fail on that count, and the woman suffers some more.

'Three, I want horses for myself and Miss Dreyfus just as soon as me and my brothers are ready to ride — and safe passage outa town. Fail on that, and the woman dies, painful as we can make it. Yuh hearin' me loud and clear there?'

'Rat!' growled Doc.

'I hear yuh,' called Malley from the depths of the boardwalk.

'And?' shouted Mason.

'Yuh got it.'

'Frank,' despaired Doc, 'what the hell yuh sayin'?'

'Do we have any choice right now?' groaned Malley. 'We need time.'

'We need a miracle more like!'

'All right,' called Mason again, 'now yuh back off. Right off. Me and the lady here don't want disturbin' 'til sun-up. We got other more intimate matters to attend to.'

'Sonofabitch!' croaked Doc, clamping his pipe to his mouth.

★　★　★

'Plain enough, ain't it? Don't need none of that spellin' out. Town's goin' to close down like night. We'd best cut our losses and leave.' Chad Lawton ran a hand over his sticky face and helped himself to another measure from the bottle on the table at his side. 'What yuh reckon?' he asked, turning to where Miras Carter relaxed in the depths of a chair in a corner of the room at the Plainsman.

Carter's grin broke slowly, slyly. 'In a hurry to get to pullin' out, ain't yuh, Chad?' he said quietly. 'Tut-tut . . . that ain't very manly of yuh, is it, specially when you're reckonin' on leavin' a lady in distress?'

Lawton threw the drink to the back of his throat, screwed his eyes, slapped his lips and thudded the glass to the table. 'Since when has Geraldine Dreyfus been a lady,' he scoffed, 'and when was she ever in distress? Don't give me that line, Carter. You know her well as I do. She's all for Geraldine Dreyfus, first and last. Step across her path at your peril.'

He shifted his gaze back to the window. 'She'll play Duke Mason like he was a fish to her hook for just as long as it suits. And we, she'll figure, can go to hell. She ain't goin' to get outa Mason's clutches. She ain't even goin' to try if all it means is fallin' foul of the sheriff. Frypan to fire just ain't the woman's style, and you know it.'

Carter steepled his fingers at the point of his chin. 'So, yuh reckon we leave, cut our losses, as you say, grab ourselves some fresh mounts and ride? That it? Not a dollar to our name? And where, pray, are we ridin' to, exactly?'

'God knows; any place yuh like. North, south . . . You name it. Just so long as we ain't around when the rest of the Mason gang hits town. That's when the lead'll start flyin', and it won't be one bit fussed where it comes to rest.'

'Whole place'll be mayhem.'

'You bet,' nodded Lawton.

Carter collapsed the steeple of fingers, and slapped his knees. 'Which is precisely what I'm gamblin' on,' he smiled.

★ ★ ★

'Troubled, Mr Mason? I do believe you are. My, my, things must be going awry. Perhaps I can help. Do feel free to ask.' Geraldine Dreyfus flashed a wickedly sardonic smile at Duke Mason as she crossed the hotel room, seated herself at the dressing-table and patted absently at her hair.

Mason cleared the sweat from his face on the sleeve of his shirt and pushed himself away from the wall. 'Kind of you, I'm sure,' he mocked, taking a slow turn round the room, his gaze suddenly distant and thoughtful.

'I would hazard a guess that the trouble your boys appear to have encountered in Campsville was not in the planning. Right?' The woman continued to tend her hair, watchful of Mason's movement reflected in the mirror. 'I think so,' she added. 'Nothing you cannot handle, I'm sure.'

'Will yuh just latch them lips of yours?' snapped Mason. 'I'm thinkin'.'

'Well, I can see that, and I hope it's not too painful!' The woman's smile shimmered. 'The answer, of course, is obvious.'

Mason moved closer to the woman's back. 'Yuh reckon? So you're goin' to tell me, eh?'

'If you wish.'

'Go right ahead.'

Geraldine Dreyfus stiffened and settled her hands in her lap. 'No disputing the fact that Sheriff Malley and a whole posse of sworn deputies are going to halt your men the minute they hit town. And rest assured he will have the stronger hand, if only to the value of sheer numbers. So your boys will be jailed — or dead — almost before breakfast.'

Mason licked his lips.

'That,' the woman continued, 'will leave you high and dry, Mr Mason;

stranded and forced to back down sooner or later. Sooner, I suspect.' She paused, her fingers reaching to idle over the handle of a hairbrush. 'Unless, of course, you make a move *before* your men hit Jackson. Before sun-up.' She paused again. 'You have about an hour, I would think.'

Mason's stare into the mirror, deep and directly into Geraldine Dreyfus's eyes, narrowed and hardened. 'And just what sort of a move am I supposed to be makin'?'

'Sheriff Malley will not be figuring on your doing anything before first light. It will not be difficult, I suspect, to sneak away from here, help yourself to a horse — there'll be no shortage in all the activity — and be long gone in well under the hour.'

'And you?' asked Mason. 'Where will you be while all this is goin' on?'

'Why, right there at your side, of course,' smiled the woman, lifting the brush to her hair. 'You are surely not planning to leave Jackson completely empty-handed?'

'Just what in the name of hell — ' began Mason.

The woman's voice sharpened. 'Think it through: Malley's got most of the bank guards under his control. Chances are Louis Quainsley will be in his private quarters almost alone, and I, Mr Mason, have a guaranteed access to him at any time I choose. Believe me, we shall be able to help ourselves.

In fifteen minutes from the point of entry, we could be collecting enough money to keep us both in extreme comfort for the rest of our days.'

Geraldine Dreyfus paused, her gaze through the mirror set like a beam on Duke Mason's face. 'You now have fifty minutes before first light. And time, Mr Mason, does not wait.'

20

Frank Malley heaved a long sigh of relief, looked a touch circumspectly at the fresh bandages binding his shoulder wound, grunted and slid an arm into his shirt.

'You'll do,' said Doc Baynam, drying his hands on a towel. 'T'ain't right yet, but it's mendin'. Just don't go strainin' it, yuh hear?'

'Oh, sure,' said Malley on a wry grin. 'I'll just sit round the next few hours, eh? Go take m'self a quiet stroll.' He sighed again. 'Sorry, Doc, didn't mean to sound ungrateful.' He finished dressing. 'Thanks.'

'Yeah, well,' murmured Doc, 'you go easy there. Ain't goin' to be no use to yourself or this town if yuh get to feelin' bitter. We got too much on our plate right now. Which reminds me . . .'

He crossed quickly to the window in

the sheriff's office and peered into the still night-black, shadowed street where only the minimum of lantern light crept over the boardwalks. 'Had me a suspicion I saw that fella Lawton nosyin' around out there. You reckon we should settle him and Carter some place we can keep a closer watch?'

'Can't keep everybody under lock and key, Doc,' said Malley. 'Goin' to have to trust to our own men stayin' wide awake.' He adjusted the set of his gunbelt. 'Meantime, I'm a whole sight more interested in the Mason gang's arrival.'

'The sonofabitch holed up there at the Palace seems to be callin' all the shots,' grunted Doc. 'Hell, how do you reckon that woman's goin' to handle him?'

'I figure for her bein' a whole sight more resourceful than most might be in her situation. Trouble is, I just daren't close in with Mason in the mood he is. He knows he's holdin' an ace card, and he'll play it given the spit of an excuse. So I guess — '

The door to the office opened ahead of a flurry of limbs, thudding boots and a sweat-stained, grime-streaked face. 'We got trouble, Frank,' gasped a newly sworn deputy, still clinging to the doorknob. 'Fire! Back of Miss Peabody's bonnet store. It's gettin' a hold. Goin' to need all the hands we can get.'

'Do what yuh can, fast as yuh can,' ordered Malley. 'Tell Carbonne I want all the staff he can spare — guests he's holdin' at the Plainsman along of 'em: Anybody, f'Cris'sake! And tell the judge to threaten the force of the law to them as ain't co-operative. Oh, and get Polly Sweet to look to Miss Peabody.'

'Ain't nobody seen Poll in hours,' said the deputy.

'All right, all right. Leave it with me. You just shift. We're followin'.'

The deputy scurried away to the steadily filling street as Malley turned to Doc. 'Grab what yuh goin' to need, Doc, and get to the store. Find out what's happened to Polly.'

'Where you goin'?' asked Doc, throwing cloths and bandages into his bag.

'Palace and then the Plainsman. This fire ain't no accident. It's deliberate, and for a purpose.' Malley's eyes narrowed in a long stare into Doc's face. 'Mebbe yuh were right, Doc. Mebbe yuh did see Lawton out there.'

'And the Mason gang?' swallowed Doc.

Malley ran a hand over his face. 'Don't even ask. Let's move!'

★   ★   ★

Polly Sweet dragged a sheet from the bed to cover her nakedness and padded quickly across the plush carpeted floor of Louis Quainsley's private apartment above the bank to the window where the drapes were only partially drawn.

'Hell!' she murmured, her moon-eyed gaze taking in the licking flames at the millinery store, the glowing, smoke-smudged sky and the bustling main street. 'Yuh seen this?' she called on a quick glance to the ante-room where Quainsley was struggling into his clothes. 'Miss Peabody's place is goin' up.'

'I know,' answered Quainsley, 'I seen it.' He cursed quietly as he pulled on his pants. 'Smelled the smoke. Just about to slip in side of yuh there . . . Damnit! Sorry about this, Poll. Yuh'll get yuh money same as usual.'

'Thanks, I'm sure,' muttered Polly indifferently, her gaze still on the flames and the activity in the street.

'Best get myself down there,' huffed Quainsley, 'see what's to be done. I tell yuh straight up, Poll, world's goin' mad, leastways goin' crazy here in Jackson. I ain't never seen or known a time like it. Why, damn it, we go on like this there won't *be* a town!' He cursed again. 'What's goin' on down there? Can yuh see?'

'See enough,' said Polly, craning to

left and right. 'Malley's new deputies have taken charge. Most of your fellas there too. Looks as if they're bringin' the fire under control. Whole chain of water pails in use. Must be half the town down there. Can see Doc Baynam, and the judge. Ain't no sign of Frank Malley.'

'If that lawman of ours has got half a brain he'll be watchin' for them Mason boys ridin' in. Can yuh see what's happenin' at the Palace? Hell, if Duke Mason gets away with Miss Drey-fus . . . '

'He won't,' said Polly, peering closer. 'He ain't stupid enough to try that, fire or no fire. He'll figure for Malley watchin' for him.'

'Yeah, well, hope you're right. Last thing we want . . . What the hell's with this cravat, f'Cris'sake?'

'Yuh ain't goin' to a banquet, Louis,' called Polly. 'What yuh want with a cravat, in heaven's name? Ain't nobody goin' to notice.'

'You'd be surprised, young lady,' said

Quainsley, crossing into the main room, the cravat twisted at his neck, fingers fumbling through it. 'Folk notice detail at the most amazin' times. Why, I recall . . . Can yuh do somethin' with this cravat, Poll?'

Polly turned from the window, let the sheet slide to the floor, took the ends of the cravat in her hands, and tied it.

'There,' she smiled approvingly. 'Yuh look just fine, Mr Bank President!'

Louis Quainsley swallowed, grabbed his hat and coat and hurried to the door. 'Do put something on, Polly,' he gulped, disappearing in a swirl of arms and legs.

'Bankers,' groaned Polly, crossing to her own clothes scattered in a chair, 'sometimes they ain't worth a bent quarter!'

★ ★ ★

Duke Mason put a finger to his lips for silence, waited a moment in the deepest shadows of the corridor, listened carefully, then gestured for Geraldine Dreyfus to close the door to the hotel room, and slip to his side.

'So far, so good,' he whispered, taking a firmer grip on the drawn Colt as he pressed his shoulders to the wall and took the woman's hand in his. 'Easy,' he murmured, 'and stay close. Not a sound.'

The woman blinked, nodded and slid a step tighter.

Mason moved on down the corridor, the woman tracking his every step, her hand warm and anxious in his. He ducked carefully under a flickering light, paused again, listened, the Colt raised, shoulders straight and firm.

'Straight ahead,' he hissed, indicating the door at the shadowed end of the corridor.

Geraldine Dreyfus froze for a moment at the sound of a door opening and closing somewhere below them.

Mason flashed her a glance and put

the barrel of the Colt to his lips.

Footsteps crossing the reception area; two men heading for the stairs to the rooms. Mason licked at sweat. The woman's hand was suddenly damp in his grip.

'Don't move, not a muscle,' he whispered.

'All looks secure enough down here,' called one of the men from the foot of the stairs. 'Want me to take a look up top?'

'Any sounds?' asked his partner.

'No sounds, no movements. All quiet.'

'Good enough. We'll be a damn sight more useful fightin' that fire. Let's shift.'

'Yuh got it.'

Footsteps heading back across the reception area; door opening again, closing; footfalls fading.

'That's it,' hissed Mason. 'Now we shift, and fast.' He drew the woman closer. 'Yuh looked a mite scared there,' he grinned.

'I was a mite scared, Mr Mason. I make no bones about it. All right now, though.'

Mason grunted. 'I figure for that door there openin' on the back stairs. What yuh reckon?'

'It does. I checked it before.'

Mason raised an eyebrow. 'Resourceful lady, eh? I like it. Right, so that's our way out. Real quiet still and no rushin'. I'm just bankin' on that fire keepin' everybody occupied. Two minutes and we'll be clear. What about the bank?'

'You can leave that side of things to me.'

Mason grunted again. 'Yuh figure for yuh friends startin' the fire?' he asked, his gaze tight on the door.

'Don't you?' said the woman.

'Grateful for the diversion, but it means they're still in town, don't it? Means they ain't abandoned their plans completely.'

Geraldine Dreyfus's eyes darkened. 'We're wastin' time. Open that door.'

* ★ ★

Miras Carter swung his gaze across the sprawl of the glow through the deep night sky. Highly satisfactory he thought. Lawton had done a good job. Enough of a blaze back there at the millinery to keep the townsfolk, and the law, occupied for hours.

He followed the track of a line of shooting sparks before it broke in a showering veil. Colourful too, he mused, if you looked at it that way. Not that the old lady who owned the store would be seeing it quite so colourfully. He would make a mental note to ensure she was suitably recompensed. Anonymously, of course. Only decent thing to do.

He hunched himself deeper into his jacket, tapped the butt of his Colt and scanned the street beyond the alley. Still hectic out there; folk coming and going. No sign of the sheriff. He would need to know his exact whereabouts.

A dark figure drifted towards him

from the shadows.

'Yuh all set?' whispered Lawton, coming closer. 'Quainsley's left the bank. Mebbe a guard there, two at most. Nothin' we can't handle. Shall we move? We need to be clear before first light.'

'We move. Stay with the shadows. No talkin', and don't hurry it. Horses?'

'Two hitched back of the bank. Saddled and ready to ride.'

Carter grinned and rubbed his hands together. 'That'll do very well, Mr Lawton, very well. Now let's go rob ourselves a bank!'

21

Doc Baynam mopped his brow with an already damp bandanna, eased the band of his hat and narrowed his eyes against the haze of the flames.

'We got the measure of it now, Doc,' said a man supervising the chain gang of town men fighting the blaze. 'Another half-hour and it'll be down to smoke and embers.' He mopped at his own brow. 'Damn shame. Who the hell'd wanna do a thing like this to Miss Peabody? Poor soul wouldn't have the heart to swat a fly. If I get my hands on the sonofabitch — '

'And yuh might at that,' coughed Doc, as the fire smoke swirled on the thin breeze.

'You bet,' smiled the man. 'Still,' he added, the smile disappearing on a sudden lunge of shadow, 'there's somethin' beginnin' to spook about this town. Yuh get that feelin', Doc?'

'Know what yuh mean.' Doc pocketed the bandanna and picked up his medicine bag. 'See Sheriff Malley there. I'll go join him. There's things to get to before sun-up.'

'Them Mason boys for one thing, eh?' said the man. 'Talk is as how they're ridin' in outa Campsville. That a fact?'

'It's a fact,' sighed Doc. 'No point in hidin' it.'

'We'll be waitin', don't you fret. Soon as we got this sorted, there ain't a man who ain't ready and willin' — '

'I hear yuh,' grinned Doc, 'but you just go easy. Family man, ain't yuh? Didn't I deliver that last boy of yours?'

'Sure did, Doc, and a fine lad he is at that. Even so, Jackson's our home, ain't it? Damn it, we built it, plank for plank. I know, I was here when it weren't no more than dust and dirt and rattlers. I ain't for havin' my life's work fouled by no Mason gang trash — that rat holed-up with the woman at the Palace bein' a priority.'

'No,' said Doc quietly, 'I guess yuh ain't at that.' He shrugged into his jacket. 'See yuh around. And thanks.'

Doc turned his back on the crackling hisses and billowing smoke and stepped quickly along the street to join Frank Malley.

'How's it lookin'?' he asked. 'Yuh men in position?'

'All doin' as they're supposed to be doin',' said Malley. 'Now it's just a matter of time.'

'Mason and Miss Dreyfus?'

'All quiet. Light still burnin' in their room. I'm on my way to the Palace right now. Any sign of Lawton and Carter? No, there wouldn't be, o'course. Stayin' low if they've got any sense. What about Polly?'

'One of her girls tells me she had a message from Quainsley earlier tonight. Last seen headin' for the bank. Still there, I'd reckon, though I seen Quainsley on the prowl.'

'I'll look in there too,' said Malley.

'We seal this end of town, then turn the concentration on the main trail from the north. That's where we'll catch our first sight of the Masons.'

'Halt the scum right there, and take 'em in. That the plan?'

'Sounds easy if yuh say it fast, don't it?'

Malley hitched his gunbelt and moved away to the shadows, gazing quickly over the night sky to the east as he went.

Smudge of grey light there, he thought, without daring to give it a second glance.

*   *   *

Polly Sweet was fully dressed, the folds of her long skirt smoothed into place, her hair tied neatly into her neck and the shawl she always wore against the night chill flung casually across her shoulders, when she hesitated, her hands on the doorknob and listened carefully, closely, for the sound she would have sworn she had heard in the sprawling labyrinth of the bank below her.

One of the guards, she wondered, pressing her ear against the door? Had to be. Quainsley had insisted on two remaining on patrol. Even so, the noise had sounded somehow very like something she had heard before: two bits to a tot of bad sourmash very like a body thudding to the floor. Heck, she had seen and heard enough of them in her time!

So had a guard taken to the bottle, she pondered? He was in for a rude and razor-edge awakening if he had; Quainsley would hound him out of town.

She pressed closer to the door. Too damned quiet by a half out there. Not natural. What had happened to the second guard? Or maybe he was covering for his drunken partner, dragging him out of sight some place.

She would go take a look, she decided, but turn a blind eye if she crossed anything untowards. Damn it, most of the bank guards were her customers. That was it, turn a blind eye, get out, back to business, but not before looking to Miss Peabody who must be in a state of near exhaustion by now.

Polly stood back, swallowing a gasp, as the doorknob began to turn.

* * *

Frank Malley drifted quietly away from the busy main street and the half-lit boardwalks where men were still gathered in small, nervous groups, some helping in the fight against the fire, some casting anxious glances at the deserted Palace Hotel with its single light at a single window, others simply there because it would have been impossible to sleep anyhow.

Maybe he should have imposed a curfew, he thought, closed the town down. But, then, he had not reckoned on the fire, and the problems with curfew were that you needed an army of men and some top shootists to hold it. He had neither.

He passed quickly by the Plainsman, where Carbonne and Judge McArthur could be heard to be in charge, crossed through a darkened patch of the street and was into the clutter at the rear of the Palace within seconds, the glow of the store fire high in the sky at his back.

All quiet here too, he thought, wondering if his patrolling deputies might be close. He would enter by the back door and do his own inspection of the premises; maybe try again to talk some sense into Mason, at least check on the woman, make certain she was safe and still in one piece.

It was the swish of what might have been fabric, perhaps the rustle of the folds of a long skirt, that halted Malley mid-step.

He waited, hand on holstered Colt, body tensed, the shoulder wound throbbing, his gaze tight and fixed on the darkness ahead of him.

'Anybody there?' he hissed, just loud enough to be heard. 'That you, Poll?'

He had moved, taken a step closer to the door, when a grey smudge across the shadows took on a shape: a body, shoulders, sprawl of hair, and then a face.

'Miss Dreyfus?' frowned Malley, relaxing. 'Just how in hell have yuh managed — '

But that was as far as Malley's question got, drowning as it did in a croaking choke, a swirl of light that flashed a maze of distorted shapes across his eyes, a final blinding rush of stars, to end in a silent, emptying darkness as the sheriff slid to the dirt and Duke Mason twirled his Colt through his fingers and back to its holster.

'Should sleep like a babe,' he grinned, waiting for Geraldine Dreyfus to come to his side again and take his hand in hers.

'Long enough for us to get rich?' she asked on a sparkling glance.

'Guaranteed, ma'am. Guaranteed!'

★　★　★

'Yuh back right up there, gal, no messin'.' Chad Lawton threatened the Colt's barrel menacingly at Polly Sweet's stomach as he prodded her deeper into the room. 'You'll come to no harm if yuh do as you're told. You got my word on it.'

'Bet that ain't worth more than a holed boot!' scoffed Polly, backing from the door.

Lawton merely grinned and grunted, his gaze moving quickly over the lavishly furnished, expensively decorated private quarters. 'My, my,' he murmured, 'Quainsley does himself proud, eh? Classy, and costly. What money buys, eh?' His gaze settled on Polly. 'You come with the trimmings, gal, or does the president rent yuh by the hour?'

Polly twisted her lips round a scowl. 'Yuh ain't in the same corral, mister, not even close. And I'd figure for yuh bein' way outa yuh depth here. How'd yuh get in anyhow?'

'Side door to the stores room left

unlocked in the mayhem out there. And only two guards. Simple as that. Even bank presidents get to lapsin' — in more ways than one, it seems!' grinned Lawton, winking at Polly, then turning as Miras Carter stepped quickly into the room, a Colt gripped uneasily in his right hand.

'Guards won't be givin' us no trouble,' said Carter. 'So what's with her?' he muttered, glancing at Polly. 'We ain't no place for loose bodies clutterin' the place. Get rid of her. Time's pressin'.'

'Charlie Baker's back room, Denver. Three years ago come Fall,' snapped Polly. 'I just remembered.'

'What yuh lippin' on about there, lady?' frowned Carter.

'Charlie Baker's place. Cheap-Jack gaming-house. Night yuh shot Johnny Rents and tried to rape me. You recall, Mr Carter?' Polly relaxed on one hip and folded her arms. 'Ain't moved on a deal, have yuh? Still down there with the rats!'

Carter tensed, his grip on the Colt whitening his knuckles. 'Give me a whole heap of pleasure to take yuh out myself, ma'am.' His grin slanted to a corner of his mouth. 'In fact, I think I'll do just that — '

'Hold it!' hissed Lawton from where he stood at the open door. 'I think we got company.'

Polly swallowed on a knotted stomach. Carter licked his lips, watching Lawton like a nervous buzzard.

'Duke Mason,' hissed Lawton again.

Carter's eyes narrowed. 'Geraldine with him?'

'She's with him. Must've come in by the same route we took.' Lawton edged a half-step nearer the shadowed corridor beyond the door. 'You want I should deal with Mason?'

'Do it, and make it fast. Watch out for Geraldine.'

'Shot's goin' to bring half the town down on our heads,' said Lawton. 'Yuh reckonin' for that, ain't yuh?'

'Let 'em come — whole darned town

if need be. We got the whore here. She'll be our free ride clear.' Carter's grin slanted again.' Now let's get this over with and come to the serious business of money. Go kill Duke Mason, will yuh?'

Polly Sweet blinked on the half-lit gloom and began to shiver.

22

'Hell!' cursed Duke Mason on a hiss of strangled breath as he tripped across the bloodstained body of a bank guard. 'We ain't the first here, lady.'

Geraldine Dreyfus pulled irritably at the shawl across her shoulders and side-stepped the unconscious man with a look of disdain. 'He dead?' she murmured.

'Not quite,' said Mason, squinting into the sprawling space of the bank's interior. 'His partner's over there. Similar condition. Somebody's been busy. Your friends Carter and Lawton?'

The woman moved ahead. 'Who cares? We're here for only one thing. Let's get to it.'

'If you're plannin' on blowin' a safe — '

'Nothin' so primitive. There's a private room back of Quainsley's office where the old miser keeps a personal hoard in cash, bonds, jewellery — money he takes from the poor souls who are struggling on loan repayments. I've seen it. He showed me. This way.'

'How come he got to showin' yuh?' croaked Mason.

'Because he's vulnerable and a fool, same as most men. Now, come on. This is not a picnic outing — '

'Too right it ain't — but whatever, it's over for you, Mason.'

The voice cracked across the gloom as if splintering it and only seconds ahead of the slow, careful click of a gun hammer.

'Evenin', Geraldine,' drawled Lawton, stepping from the twist of ornate stairway to a pool of pale half light. His slow, cat-like grin lit his eyes as they settled on Mason. 'Nothin' rash there, Duke. Yuh might regret it, and you've been *vulnerable* and *fool* enough already by the look of it.'

'Now yuh hold on there,' gestured Mason.

'No time,' said Lawton. 'We're racin' against the clock. But before I kill yuh, just to say thanks for deliverin' Miss Dreyfus safe and sound. Miras Carter'll be obliged, I'm sure.'

'Hang on there,' began Mason again, glancing frantically at Geraldine Dreyfus. 'Well, tell him, f'Cris'sake. Tell him how I got yuh out of that hotel room, how I've taken care of that nosyin' sheriff. Tell him!'

The woman shrugged and began to move away to the door of Quainsley's office. 'Just do it, Lawton. Talking can get to being expensive round here.'

'What the hell, yuh two-timin' bitch!' blustered Mason, at the same time launching himself face on into the bulk of Lawton.

The primed Colt spat, but the shot whined high into the ceiling. Lawton cursed, tried to come back to the line of his crashing target; too late, their bodies thudded together, his Colt flew free and arms and legs twisted in a threshing mêlée, groans, grunts and smashing fists breaking the silence.

Geraldine Dreyfus had hurried on to the office, tried the door, cursed aloud at finding it locked, and turned back to the struggling bodies when Miras Carter appeared in the shadows at the top of the stairs.

'Geraldine,' he called, 'what in the devil's name is goin' on down there?'

'We need to get into Quainsley's office,' she called back, as Lawton and Mason struggled to their feet, their fists still flying. 'It's locked, damn it.'

'Hold on,' snapped Carter, unaware in those seconds of Polly Sweet drifting as if a mist from the private quarters, the neck of a cut-glass decanter firmly in her grip.

'Back of you!' yelled Geraldine Dreyfus.

Carter swung round, an arm raising instinctively as the decanter began its fateful downward rush to smash across his arm and the top of his head in a shower of shards, spurting an instant stream of blood into his eyes.

He half screamed, groaned, swung round again, lost his footing and bearing and spun into a headlong crash down the stairs.

Polly Sweet raced after him. Geraldine Dreyfus backed towards Quainsley's office.

Lawton grunted as he flung a wild punch, missed Mason's face and stumbled into the gunslinger's raised knee. He sprawled across the floor, groaned under the force of Mason's boot crashing across his neck and was probably near unconscious when Mason drew his Colt and blazed it once, twice through vicious licks of flame.

Mason swung round in a lather of sweat and blood, his eyes glowing with anger. 'Get back here, woman!' he screamed at Geraldine Dreyfus, before swinging the gleaming gun barrel on the spreadeagled body of Miras Carter and drilling a single shot into his thigh without seeming to so much as blink.

His gaze fixed on Polly Sweet. 'Who

the hell are you?' he croaked. 'What yuh want here?'

'I was — ' shivered Polly.

'Get rid of her!' snapped Geraldine Dreyfus from the thinning shadows as the first touch of light began to spread. 'Kill her — now!'

'Mebbe it's you I should be killin', lady,' grated Mason, the sweat dripping from him like rain. 'Yuh were quick enough there to have Lawton finish me.'

'That was all — '

But Geraldine Dreyfus's words were lost in a sudden piercing burst of gunfire, yells, pounding hoofs, snorting horses, jangling tack and creaking, cracking leather.

'Sounds like the boys have hit town,' grinned Mason. 'And right on time too!'

★ ★ ★

'We're losin' it, Frank, damned if we aren't! Whole town's set'n' into panic.'

Doc Baynam wiped a hand across his face as he steadied Sheriff Malley on his uncertain legs and eased him into a standing position against the wall of a tumbledown shack. 'Hell, Mason sure gave yuh some sore head there. Just what yuh needed, eh? Like yuh need gut-rot!'

'What's the situation, Doc?' groaned Malley, blinking to focus his gaze on the strengthening dawn light.

'Well, we got the fire at Miss Peabody's under control. It's out, but the Masons are here,' said Doc examining the back of the sheriff's head. 'Slipped in unseen. Must've come down on that old trail outa Dead Creek, wrong side of where Mac Downie was watchin'. Anyhow, they're here — as if yuh can't hear 'em! — but only three: Jacob, Charlie Drace and Zeb Crow. Matt ain't with 'em.'

Malley winced and blinked again. 'Go on,' he croaked.

'Seems like Duke Mason and the Dreyfus woman headed for the bank from here — only to find Chad Lawton and Miras Carter already there. Talk about settin' up a nest of thievin' vipers!' Doc sighed and reached into his bag for a clean bandage. 'Know somethin' — it's a whole sight of a blessin' for you I came in search of yuh and happened along this way.'

'Sure, sure, and I'm grateful yuh did,' soothed Malley impatiently. 'Where are the rats holed up now? Still at the bank?'

'Seems like it. Duke Mason appears to be in charge, so there's no sayin' what's happened to Lawton and Carter. Dreyfus woman must be there, but so is Polly Sweet, leastways accordin' to Quainsley.' Doc grunted. 'Apparently she was still dressin' when he left.'

'Damn it!' snapped Malley.

'My figurin' reckons on the Masons helpin' themselves to what they can lift from the bank and usin' the two women as hostages to broker their way outa town.'

'No chance,' snapped Malley again.

'Oh, and who's goin' to stop 'em?'

'We are, Doc, you and me. You go round up them deputies of mine and get 'em positioned front and back of the bank. Every man armed and ready to shoot the minute he has a clear target. Any other town fella wants to join 'em, let him. You're in charge. And, f'Cris'sake, keep Quainsley, Carbonne and the judge under control. Yuh got all that?'

''Course I have,' said Doc, closing his bag with a thud. 'And I ain't even goin' to ask where you'll be, 'cus I already know!'

'Just so long as we understand each other, eh, Doc?' winked Malley.

★ ★ ★

Polly Sweet stepped slowly, carefully backwards, conscious of reaching the bank counter and the distance it would place between herself and the bodies, dead and alive, cluttering the floor space.

She swallowed on a creek-bed throat, dry as dirt and tight as old stone, ran her hands down her skirt and shifted her gaze quickly from Geraldine Dreyfus, where she hovered awkwardly at the door to Quainsley's office, to the lifeless bulk of Chad Lawton and the near-dead body of Carter, then to Duke Mason and his sidekicks.

'Yuh been busy, Brother,' grinned Jacob approvingly. 'And we're addin' females to the haul, I see.'

'Where's Matt?' snapped Duke, his Colt still firm in his grip. 'Why ain't he here along of yuh, and what's with you fellas lookin' like trail trash? What's been goin' on?'

'We crossed a spot of bother back at Campsville,' murmured Zeb Crow. 'It turned nasty.'

'I heard some such talk from the lawman here,' snapped Duke again, his eyes gleaming. 'It true? Matt get himself in a shoot-out?' He slapped the barrel of the Colt against his thigh. 'Don't tell me that fool hit the bottle again?'

'Just that,' murmured Charlie Drace from the shadows. 'Shot three men, one of them a deputy.'

'But where's he now, f'Cris'sake?' persisted Duke. 'Why ain't he here?'

''Cus he's dead, that's why,' blurted Jacob, beginning to sweat.

Duke's gaze darkened. 'How? The sheriff back at Campsville take him out? Who killed him? *Who, damn it?*'

There were seconds then when Polly Sweet swallowed and simply stared, when Geraldine Dreyfus seemed as immobile as a bulk of granite and Duke Mason's gaze across the faces of his gang hardened to the sharpness of flint.

'I did,' said Charlie Drace almost casually as he eased aside to place a shaft of light through the bank's windows directly behind him. 'He drew on me in liquor. It'd been comin', and it was quick.'

'S'right,' spluttered Zeb Crow, wiping the back of his hand across his matted stubble. 'I saw the whole darned thing. Right there in them trail rocks. Matt had drunk himself somethin' rotten. True he had, Duke. Why, if you'd seen him — '

Duke Mason's Colt blazed at close range, spilling Zeb Crow's gut blood as if puncturing a pail, throwing the man back until his heels fouled on the body of Chad Lawton and he crashed to the floor without so much as a moan.

'I don't wanna hear no more about liquor and rocks and . . . Goddamnit, that was my brother yuh murdered back there, Charlie Drace,' hissed Mason, thrusting the Colt's aim at Drace, his gaze dancing crazily. 'And you can bet on yourself goin' the same way as yuh scumbag partner there, right now — '

'Hold on, Brother, hold on,' spluttered Jacob, his face a sudden sponge of sweat and grime and pitted trail dirt in which his eyes glazed like broken glass. 'What we doin' f'Cris'sake? Just what are we doin'? Goin' crazy? We've lost Matt — and he walked into that, Duke, believe me — and now, in hell's name, yuh just shot Zeb in cold blood. He weren't doin' no wrong; no, just tryin' to explain, that's all. And, goddamnit, here we are in one of the country's biggest, richest banks . . . It's ours! So tell me, *what are we doing?*'

Polly Sweet shuddered and backed noisily into the bank counter under Charlie Drace's withering glance. Geraldine Dreyfus tried to ease deeper into the shadows at the office door.

'You stay right where yuh are, lady,' spat Duke. 'Another step, and believe me I ain't goin' to be one mite fussed about killin' yuh.'

'Too good-lookin' to waste,' murmured Drace, his gaze like a sheet of ice on the shivering, wan-faced woman.

'We're wastin' time,' said Jacob, licking at hot sweat, anxious now to smother his brother's anger. 'Where's the money? Let's get to it and get out. We'll use the women as a shield.'

'Yuh givin' any thought to what's likely to be out there?' asked Drace, glancing quickly at Jacob but holding his stare on Duke. 'I'd figure for best part of the town bein' lined up. Primed guns just waitin'.'

'So?' shrugged Jacob, still licking. 'Like I say, we got the women. Ain't no gun goin' to spit against a woman — not even in Jackson.'

'There's them bank guards. Zeb knew all about them,' said Drace. 'Pity yuh had to go killin' him,' he added cynically.

'Don't you get to remindin' me again of who's double-crossin' and shootin' up who round here, Charlie Drace,' snapped Duke, gesturing with the Colt again. 'One more word outa you — '

'All right! All right!' shouted Jacob. 'Let's just get to doin' what we do best, shall we, f'Cris'sake?'

'*Mason, yuh there? Yuh hearin' me? Doc Baynam here.*'

The voice from the street broke across the morning like the sudden tolling of a bell.

'*You're surrounded, you know that, don't yuh? Ain't no runnin' from here.*'

Polly began to tremble and press herself into the counter. Geraldine Dreyfus twitched her fingers nervously over her clothes.

'Yuh got just three minutes to get y'self and whoever's still alive out here. No guns, no messin'. Three minutes, and then we're comin' in — all twenty of us!'

23

Doc Baynam blinked on the spreading haze of dawn and lit his pipe carefully. 'Best offer we can put on the table right now,' he murmured, more to himself than the wheezing bulk at his side.

'Mason ain't the type to put his tail between his legs,' said Judge McArthur, fingering the chain to his pocketed timepiece. 'More likely to come outa there all guns blazin'.' He squinted out across and along the street. Everybody in position?'

'Enough lead hereabouts to sink a steamboat,' said Doc, blowing a cloud of smoke over the thin morning air, wondering just where Frank Malley was hidden. 'It's the women that spook me,' he grunted. 'Hell, if them scum use Polly and the Dreyfus woman as a shield . . . '

'Dreyfus woman has probably

hitched up along of Mason,' wheezed the judge. 'I don't fancy for her bein' particularly loyal to anybody, savin' herself.'

Both men turned to the deeper shadows at their backs at the sound of approaching footfalls.

'I just hope them two-bit sonsofbitches ain't foulin' up my bank!' moaned Louis Quainsley on a furrowed scowl. 'I get my hands on the rats — '

'Which ain't one spit likely,' said Doc. 'I just hope yuh didn't overindulge bank information to Miss Dreyfus in there. Yuh didn't, did yuh, Louis?'

Quainsley's gaze was suddenly hollowed and vague.

* * *

'Well,' muttered Jacob Mason, 'so what do we do now, big brother? We goin' to make a break for it?' The gunslinger mopped his grubby face on his shirt sleeve. 'I'm tellin' yuh now, Duke — '

'You ain't tellin' me nothin', Jacob,' returned Duke from the side of the window overlooking the street. 'Yuh just gettin' on my nerves with all your moanin' talk.' He shot the man a fierce glance. 'So sit on it, will yuh?' He nodded to Drace. 'What yuh figure, Charlie, we grab what we can and hightail it?'

'We do just that — and fast — and before we get to findin' out just where the law around here has buried itself.'

Mason swung his gaze to the hovering, twitching Geraldine Dreyfus. 'Yuh heard the man, so yuh get into that office and start loadin' all we can carry.' He levelled his Colt at Polly. 'You get behind the counter yuh proppin' up there and get some bags or somethin' for the lady. Shift!'

Polly trembled, forced her limbs to work, hands to come back to her sides, legs to carry her to the counter hatch, find the strength in her fingers to lift it, carefully, slowly. She moved behind the counter, conscious of Drace's eyes following her every move, switching swiftly to where Jacob gestured for Geraldine Dreyfus to stand aside as he kicked open the door to Quainsley's office.

'Let's hurry it along there,' called Duke, watching the street anxiously. 'This ain't no prayer meetin'.'

Polly's hands rummaged nervously along the shelves beneath the counter; papers, more papers, ledgers, books, box files — cotton money bags. She grabbed at a half-dozen and dragged them towards her, panicking now as Charlie Drace crossed the room.

She smiled wanly, her lips beginning to quiver, a smile that might so easily have snapped in a gasp as her fingers ran across the barrel and then the butt of a Colt.

Hell, she thought, hesitating for a split second, she must have rummaged through the area where a counter clerk kept a weapon as a last resort of deterrent against unwelcome cutomers. But how . . . Supposing . . . ?

'What yuh got there, gal?' clipped Drace, reaching across the counter.

Polly lifted the bags and shoved them into the man's hands, watched him turn and stride away to the office, then reached for the Colt and slid it into her dress.

'*Time's runnin' out on yuh, Mason,*' warned Doc Baynam from across the street.

'Yuh ready yet?' hissed Mason impatiently.

'Two minutes,' returned Jacob, urging Geraldine Dreyfus to hurry in her opening and closing of drawers, boxes, cabinets.

'Hell, what's this?' frowned Drace from the doorway. 'Bank president's personal hoard?'

'Only some of it,' said the woman. 'There's more in his private quarters, but there won't be the time. This will have to do.'

'Handsome enough,' grinned Drace approvingly. 'Same goes for you, lady. Glad we met up.'

'Don't get to fooling yourself, mister.' The woman's eyes flashed. 'And just so you don't go getting ideas way out of your reach, the man bleeding to death back of you there is Miras Carter, my partner, and the brains behind a heist here that would have netted us a fortune if it hadn't been for the filth of your own and the Masons' interfering hands.' She sniffed and tossed the falls of her hair. 'What are you going to do about Mr Carter?' she snapped icily.

'Yuh want I should finish him?' shrugged Drace, his grin breaking to a cynical smile.

Jacob tittered.

The woman spat across the money and papers spread in front of her. 'Help yourselves!' she flared.

'What the hell's goin' on back there?' called Duke. 'Ain't yuh through yet?'

'Oh, sure, we're through — *all* through!' grated Geraldine Dreyfus, flouncing from the office in a flurry of dancing hair and flaring skirts, then pausing a moment before coming to the prone, bloodied but still breathing body of Carter.

She raised her face in a hell-fire glare directly into Duke Mason's eyes. 'Some gun, aren't you? Well, I hope you enjoy it, and the money. Me, I'm pulling out, right now. The atmosphere in here is decidedly stale!'

'You ain't goin' no place, lady,' sneered Mason.

'Ain't *nobody* goin' no place.'

The voice pierced the tense, tight silence of the bank like the sudden honing of a blade across a sharpening stone. The ominous, no-nonsense snap of a Winchester primed to action was enough to hold the bodies gathered in the gloomy four walls stiff and immobile, as if frozen into rock, the footfalls down the sweep of the stairs as eerie as the creaking tread of a ghost.

Polly Sweet made the first sound, something between a croak and a strangled swallow, the cold bulge of the Colt beneath her skirts seeming, she imagined, to grow heavier.

Drace eased back to the shadows. Jacob's fingers fumbled on the scattered haul as he tried to scoop what he could into his shirt.

'Leave it, f'Cris'sake!' groaned Drace.

Duke Mason simply stared at the shadowy figure moving slowly down the stairs, his grip on his Colt frozen to the butt.

Geraldine Dreyfus tossed her hair again and flounced her skirts impertinently. 'At last,' she smiled, 'the law has arrived! Good morning, Sheriff Malley. I'd almost given you up, but if you want a hand here with these scum — '

'Stand aside there, Miss Dreyfus,' said Malley, the Winchester roving through a slow arc.

'What the hell,' began Duke, lowering the Colt as if to hold it loose at his side, 'I really had figured for you bein' a whole sight — '

Duke Mason's shot was always going to be hurried and at random from the hip at a target he had still not ranged into focus. It blazed inches above

Malley's shoulder, drawing the instant response in a roar of Winchester fire that threw the gunslinger back to the wall in a heap of flying limbs and lolling head.

Geraldine Dreyfus fell against the staircase rails, her eyes wide and wet with shock. Jacob Mason lunged from Quainsley's office, his gut bulging and weighed down with cash and whatever else of any value he had been able to grab and stuff into his shirt, his Colt in a grip that waved the piece somewhere high above his head, a growl rumbling out of his throat like a train through a canyon.

Malley's rifle blazed again, this time over the grovelling form of Geraldine Dreyfus as she crawled towards him. The shot ripped into Jacob's shirt spilling the cash to the floor in a jangling, clattering heap. The man groaned, raised his stone-flat eyes and fell lifeless and face-down at the woman's heels.

Polly Sweet screamed 'Frank — to

your left!' as Charlie Drace grew out of the shadows, his already blazing gun adding to the swirling smoke, the cling of cordite.

Malley dodged towards the counters.

Polly Sweet swept across the floor, lifting her skirts for a grip on the Colt, then bringing the butt of it down with a vicious thud on Geraldine Dreyfus's head before accidentally blazing a shot into the ceiling as she tried to readjust her hold.

But it was this shot that diverted Drace's concentration just long enough for Malley to crouch low, narrow his gaze and bring the Winchester into action through a roaring burst of shots that lifted Drace clear off the floor and tossed him back, over Duke Mason's body, until in a splintering crash of windowpanes, he sprawled bleeding and dead on the boardwalk.

Judge Maitland McArthur dropped a newly lit cigar at his feet and stared open-mouthed from the far side of the street.

A gathering group of men appeared to be struck dumb. Even a hound lost its bark.

Louis Quainsley sweated, gulped, shuddered and finally groaned, 'Oh, hell.'

And Doc Baynam gazed across the growing morning light and murmured, 'You can say that again!'

24

The legend gathered momentum and spread in the following weeks and months that no one, not even the notorious Duke Mason and his hellfire gang, had been able to break the security of the Western Central and South Peaks bank at Jackson.

'We are, always have been and always will be, impregnable!' its glowing, strutting, newly frock-coated president had announced with some measure of a reaffirmed arrogance — until a softly spoken but adamant Doc Baynam had taken Louis Quainsley aside and reminded him of a few brutal facts.

'You'd best not overlook that the Mason boys, and Miras Carter and his side-slingers, got into your bank awful easy,' he had winked from behind a cloud of smoke from his pipe. 'And, my friend, the Masons might well have gotten away with a pile of unexplained assets found in *your* office had it not been for Sheriff Malley and the gutsy performance of a certain Miss Polly Sweet here. No thanks to you, Louis, that your bank's still intact and in one piece. Same goes for your personal reputation, come to that. What yuh reckon?'

Quainsley reckoned it a deal more realistically from there on and confined himself to the assurance that the bank would always be 'at the service of Jackson'.

Judge Maitland McArthur was among the first to welcome Marshal Doolan to town exactly three days after the attempted raid.

'Missed it by a whisker,' he had beamed expansively. 'Some show, eh? You should've seen it! Why, we ain't had a shoot-out like that in Jackson since . . . Since never, I guess!'

'I'm here for Miras Carter,' Doolan had said coldly. 'He still alive?'

'Just, thanks to good work by Doc

Baynam, Carter'll live to hang. That what yuh plannin'?'

'Been trailin' him through half-a-dozen territories for what seems a lifetime. He'll hang, don't you fret on it.'

'Chad Lawton's dead, but the Dreyfus woman is as alive and, well, er, as intriguin', shall we say, as ever. What yuh goin' to do about her?'

'She'll stand trial in Denver. Jail sentence, I'd reckon.'

'Shame, in a woman like that. Such a waste . . .'

Marshall Doolan's stare into the judge's face had been as icily indifferent as the silence he had maintained until he and his deputies rode out of Jackson with Carter and the woman roped to trail mounts.

Geraldine Dreyfus had flashed her smile only once as she left — at what seemed to Doc like the 'whole darned town'.

Sheriff Ben Moore recovered from his gunshot wounds to 'stand to law

244

and order' along of his deputy, Lou Winters, for many years to come, content enough to tell it straight to anyone happening through Campsville as to how they had played their part in the downfall of the Mason Gang.

Frank Malley, on the other hand, had given some serious thought through his weeks of recovery to throwing in his badge, calling it a day and leaving Jackson for some small, easy-living, sun-drenched spread out West. 'Time to rest up, get myself a shaded veranda and a long prospect to a far horizon,' he had mused to Polly Sweet, as she accompanied him on one of his late night patrols of the town.

'Damnit, how long do you think you're goin' to settle for that, man of your age and standin'?' she had snapped back. 'And yuh tell me this just when I'm gettin' to think of tradin' my gamin'-house for a respectable livin' runnin' the vacant Plainsman. Hell, Frank, I'm goin' to need a reliable fella lookin' to me . . . '

Malley had finally seen the sense in Polly's outlook and done the only thing open to him — kept his badge and married the woman!

Jackson is still Jackson, the wealthiest, sassiest town south of Laramie Peaks; still boasting the luxury of the Silver Palace hotel under the watchful eye of Bertram Carbonne, Miss Peabody's brand new millinery with the 'very latest in eastern fashions', and, of course, the dominating façade of the bank.

And, it is true, the visiting stranger might still figure for the Western Central and South Peaks being way beyond the ingenuity of anyone thinking of robbing it.

It could never be done, could it?

THE END

We do hope that you have enjoyed reading this large print book.

Did you know that all of our titles are available for purchase?

We publish a wide range of high quality large print books including:
Romances, Mysteries, Classics
General Fiction
Non Fiction and Westerns

Special interest titles available in large print are:
The Little Oxford Dictionary
Music Book, Song Book
Hymn Book, Service Book

Also available from us courtesy of Oxford University Press:
Young Readers' Dictionary
(large print edition)
Young Readers' Thesaurus
(large print edition)

For further information or a free brochure, please contact us at:
Ulverscroft Large Print Books Ltd.,
The Green, Bradgate Road, Anstey,
Leicester, LE7 7FU, England.
Tel: (00 44) **0116 236 4325**
Fax: (00 44) **0116 234 0205**

A TOWN CALLED
TROUBLESOME

John Dyson

Matt Matthews had carved his ranch out of the wild Wyoming frontier. But he had his troubles. The big blow of '86 was catastrophic, with dead beeves littering the plains, and the oncoming winter presaged worse. On top of this, a gang of desperadoes had moved into the Snake River valley, killing, raping and rustling. All Matt can do is to take on the killers single-handed. But will he escape the hail of lead?